THE IDENTITY TRAP

Can one identical twin step into the other's shoes without detection? To Melinda Grainger it is child's play. Tired and depressed from the loss of her parents and a broken love affair, she jumps at the opportunity offered, out of the blue, by her sister Melissa, who is working in Jamaica. The substitution proceeds smoothly—until her employer's wife is murdered, and her twin goes missing. Melinda finds herself trapped in her sister's identity, unable to confess the truth because of her fears for Melissa, and under suspicion of complicity in the crime. Has Melissa used her to create an alibi? Or there may be a sinister force at work, with grave dirt scattered in the beds and an unspeakable bundle hidden in a wardrobe— but even the fearful rites of Obeah must come from some human hand. The motive could be politics, hatred or just plain greed.

D1355995

THE IDENTITY TRAP

by

ISOBEL LAMBOT

W.M.

WOLVERHAMPTON PUBLIC LIBRARIES

RESERVE STOCK

LOCATION CLL

CLASS No. K

I.S.B.N.

BOOK No. 782126

INVOICE No. MO456

CHECKED

ROBERT HALE · LONDON

WOLVERHAMPTON
PUBLIC LIBRARIES

© Isobel Lambot 1978

First published in Great Britain 1978

ISBN 0 7091 6620 6

Robert Hale Limited
Clerkenwell House
Clerkenwell Green
London ECIR OHT

Printed in Great Britain by Bristol Typesetting Co. Ltd,
Barton Manor, St. Philips, Bristol

AUTHOR'S NOTE

This is a detective story without a detective. All the clues are there, and the police are present in the narrative to provide forensic evidence so that you, clever reader, may play sleuth. Can you work out who killed Felicity Dewar—and why?

ONE

The search was over: the missing woman was lying on the bright sand, sprawled out on her face like a sunbather, long blonde hair spread about her; a mass of tanned flesh in an expensive minimum of bikini; pinned down by a gleaming shaft of metal protruding from the middle of her back; unmoving; dead.

Mel Grainger forced herself to look away from the body. Staring would not bring Felicity Dewar back to life. She looked around her, at the lush vegetation tumbling down steep slopes to the tiny crescent of sand and the pure blue of the Caribbean. A secret place, accessible only from the sea, Felicity's favourite haunt, the first port of call in the search, once they found her clothes at the beach house.

Inevitably, her eyes were dragged back to the pitiful sight. They had all expected trouble: an accident or a sudden illness; had known that she might be beyond help when they found her, for the search had been mounted so late; but nothing like this. Harpoons were for spearing fish in the sea, not for letting off on dry land. How could anyone have been so careless? More than careless: callous, to leave their accidental victim to die. Felicity might have been killed instantly, but even so, it was beyond pardon to leave her there. Mel supposed they had been frightened at what they had done. . . .

The men were bending over her.

"She's stiff," said Justin, then added sharply, as his cousin reached out, "No, don't touch her, Dominic."

"She's my wife!"

"We mustn't move her. We have to fetch the police."

Dominic Dewar reeled away from the body, his hands to his face.

"God!" he exclaimed. "Can't we cover her up?"

"There are towels in the boat," Justin replied. He looked round and snapped his fingers imperiously at Mel. "In the locker. Bring them."

She fumbled with the catch, her fingers numb despite the heat of the day, not questioning the order. Justin French was the sort of man who was always obeyed. She found the towels, clambered out of the boat, and handed them to him. Deftly, he spread them over the remains of his cousin's wife. The fish spear defied all covering, glinting evilly in the sun.

Justin straightened up.

"One of us has to go for the police, Dominic. Can you handle it?"

Mel felt herself to be an unwanted third. This was a family tragedy and she had no part in it. She stared at the two cousins, because it was better than gazing at the shape shrouded in towels on the sand at their feet.

There was no family resemblance between them, although she knew that their mothers were sisters. Dominic was a large, shaggy man, with a slight stoop, and a leonine head which looked well on the dust jacket of his books. He was thirty-four but seemed older. There was even a streak of grey in his thick dark hair. His face was pale and drawn under the tan. Justin French was dark, too, but there was an intense blackness about him springing from a mixed

8

heredity, thick straight hair, heavy eyebrows, swarthy skin, contrasting oddly with his clear blue eyes. A power-pack of a man : of no more than middle height, harsh-faced, ahead of his cousin by a mere two years, and a whole world of experience.

"Yes, I can manage," Dominic muttered, and without another word stumbled back to the boat.

Mel would have followed him, but Justin put out his hand to hold her back.

"You wait here with me," he said, in a forbidding tone.

In any case, it was too late now. Dominic was heading out of the creek, to the open sea, and Port Antonio, a few miles up the coast.

"Will he be all right on his own?" she ventured. "He has had a dreadful shock."

"Better to give him something to do," Justin returned brusquely. "I didn't imagine you would like to be left here alone, either, and you would not have known where to go in Port Antonio, even assuming you could handle the boat, which I doubt."

Mel felt daunted. Justin seemed to have a remarkably poor opinion of her, but he was quite right in thinking that she would not like to be left in this remote spot with a corpse for company. It did not seem to have crossed his mind that *he* could have gone for the police, while she and Dominic kept watch beside the body. But that, she supposed, was Justin French : always organising everyone in sight.

Just as he had taken command when Dominic called him at his office in down-town Kingston with the news that Felicity had not come home. Within minutes he had it all in hand; someone to check the hospitals, another to contact the police, while he and Dominic went to the beach house, for which the missing woman had set out so many hours ago. Mel had found herself swept along, like so much baggage, screaming along the twisting roads—her first trip through the famed Blue Mountains of Jamaica, a dizzy kaleidoscope of wooded scarps, deep ravines, and crystal waterfalls, but this was no moment for sight-seeing—to reach the northern shore.

She sat down on the sand, as far away from him as her craving for living human contact would permit, despising herself for the weakness.

He stood motionless, staring out over the empty sea. Mel gazed at his back, wondering irrelevantly why she found him so disturbing. If the very idea were not absurd, she might even imagine that she was afraid of him. There was no reason to be: neither he nor any of the others suspected that she was not what she appeared to be, and that they were being deceived, nor was there need for them ever to know. Felicity's death could hardly involve her, an outsider if ever there was one. Dominic would not wish to continue with the 'research'—his fancy word for the harmless deception—and she could go back whence she had come with no one the wiser. In the face of sudden death, the whole thing seemed cheap. The joke—or at a higher level, the experiment in human behaviour—had turned sour on them.

A wave of desolation swept over her. Death and misery had haunted her these past two years, and she had hoped to escape from them by flying the Atlantic, exchanging the cold of an English December for the warmth of the Caribbean. But she was a jinx. All she had done was to bring the bad luck with her.

She told herself that she should have known that there was no easy way out. Problems had to be faced. Running away achieved nothing. Yet Dominic Dewar's offer had been tempting enough to make her forget common sense . . .

A letter, arriving out of the blue, bearing Jamaican stamps and familiar handwriting. Her sister's script, which she had thought she might never see again, for all attempts to trace Melissa had failed. Her twin. The other half of the egg from which she was hatched. Melissa and Melinda, so alike that no one save their parents could tell them apart, inseparable until the ghastly scene with their father on the morning after their twenty-first birthday. There had been no word from Melissa since she stormed out of the house, leaving a great big blank in the life of her twin. Five years of silence, the hope of reconciliation growing fainter with every month.

Then the letter, lying on the mat behind the front door, waiting for her as she entered the empty echoing house where she had lived all her life, but which, now that her parents were gone, seemed changed and unwelcoming. Melissa—bubbling over as ever, the words tumbling onto the page, skimming over the lost years—wanted her to play their old childhood game, but this time for real. She explained that she was private secretary to an American author, who now planned to write a book about identical twins who could step into each other's shoes at will. The bait was the air fare and all expenses, plus an extra week on holiday with Melissa, in return for five days' impersonation of her sister, and all this in Jamaica, where Melissa, her employer and his wife were staying at his cousin's house.

Both twins knew it could be done. All their lives they had been mistaken for each other, and during their teens had gone out of their way to dress, speak, walk alike, and

11

had shortened their names to Mel, which could apply to either of them. It had all been great sport, years ago, and Melinda was tempted. She was tired and lonely and in no condition to face Christmas on her own. Melissa was all the family she had left. She told herself that it would save no end of trouble if she went to Jamaica: there were papers to be signed, concerning the estate their parents had left, now to be divided between the two of them; decisions to be made over what to do with the house and furniture . . .

And here she was, undetected in her impersonation after three days in Justin French's house, with Melissa holed up in a hotel near Kingston, and airline tickets booked for the pair of them to fly to the Virgin Islands on Christmas Eve. All nice and easy—until the moment when they realised that Felicity Dewar was missing. Mel glanced unhappily at the still form under the towels, and willed the police to come quickly so that she might escape from Dominic Dewar and his uncomfortable cousin and resume her real self.

The whirr of a speedboat brought her to her feet, eyes straining out to sea. At first there was nothing, then out of the bright light it came, a fast, red-hulled craft, in a shower of spray. A pleasure boat, not the business-like, no-nonsense police launch she had looked for. Yet, it was circling towards them and Justin was waving. The thought came, unbidden, into her mind that he expected this boat to appear, had been waiting for it.

There was a crew of two, a black man at the helm and beside him a lighter-skinned woman. As the boat edged into the creek, Mel recognised them. She had seen them at the house: Tib Morley and his wife, Lisa. Their names were on the list, which Melissa had prepared for her, of people she was supposed to know. Tiberius Morley was a hot-shot lawyer and a close friend of Justin French.

They beached the boat, and Tib climbed out, while Lisa stared in fascinated horror at the towels and what they hid from sight.

"We met Dominic," Tib announced by way of greeting. "He said Felicity was dead."

He was tall, heavily built, hair clipped short and curling to his skull, tinged with grey at each temple, a formidable man under any circumstances, ominous now in the presence of death.

"Yes," Justin replied, with a curt gesture towards the body. "Perhaps Lisa would take Mel back to the beach house. They can wait for us there."

It was hardly a question, more a command, while at the same time, a silent message passed between the two men.

"Of course," Tib replied, and Mel found herself bundled into the speedboat. The men shoved it off into the water, Lisa started the engine and they were away. Looking back, Mel saw Justin and Tib bending over Felicity.

Lisa handled the fast craft with ease. She was younger than her husband, in her early thirties, Mel guessed, while Tib must be over forty. She had honey-coloured skin, fine features, and long black hair: not a trace of negroid blood anywhere, but definitely coloured, of some mix of the many races which had found roots in the Caribbean islands. A lovely woman, by any standards.

"Was that a harpoon?" she asked suddenly, her soft voice sharpened with shock.

Mel found her throat was dry.

"Yes," she croaked. "How could anyone be so careless?"

Lisa shot a swift glance at her, then turned her attention

13

back to piloting the boat. The creek was far behind them, and ahead was a long stretch of golden sand, fringed with clumps of bamboo and palms, and beyond it the green-clad mountains. A lovely, solitary place : no sign of habitation except in the distance a low, flat-roofed building which merged into the landscape, with only a wooden jetty running out into the sea to mark its presence.

Within minutes, they were tying up at it, scrambling out of the boat. The beach house lay at the edge of the sand, a log cabin with an immense magenta bougainvillea running riot over the roof, set in a rough garden of coarse grass and flowering bushes. A simple place, in the way that the toys of the rich are simple : a spacious lounge, shaded by a wide verandah; a couple of tiny bedrooms, with a bathroom nestling between them; a minute kitchen, and a large utility room hung with bathing costumes, scuba-diving gear, and thick towels, and lavishly equipped with changing cubicles and showers. To one side was a carport, large enough to take three cars. There were two parked in it now : Justin's and Felicity's.

The sight of her car had narrowed the search immediately : no further need to check for a road accident, to call the hospitals. It was also the end of hope : no more chance that she might have lost her memory or just gone off.

Inside the house was more evidence : Felicity's clothes, and in the kitchen the hamper in which Cook had packed lunch for her, unopened.

Lisa made for the lounge, went straight to the cupboards built into the length of one wall, and fetched out a bottle of rum. She poured into two glasses.

" What you need is a drink," she said, handing one to Mel. " I don't feel too good, myself, and I didn't see her.

14

You did. Talk about it if it helps."

She walked out onto the verandah, Mel trailing after her. They dropped into rattan chairs, and gazed out over the beach and the empty sea. The heat of the day was passing, the shadows of the palms on the bright sand lengthening. Soon would come the brief tropical twilight, and then the warm, sweet-smelling darkness.

Mel choked a little on the raw spirit, but soon felt an inner comfort spreading through her, for there was a chill in the marrow of her bones which defied climate. The numbness which had seized her brain from the moment that she glimpsed Felicity's body gradually left her.

"She must have been there since sometime yesterday," she said, blurting out the first thought that came to her. "We should have found her sooner."

Lisa looked at her.

"Why didn't you?" she asked bluntly.

It was a question everyone would pose: how it was that a member of a family could be missing for so many hours before anyone mounted a search. The answer lay in strained relationships and in the dead woman's personality. Melissa had described her employer's wife as a Grade A bitch, and Mel's own brief experience of her confirmed the judgement. It was hardly the right moment to voice such a home truth.

"Mr. Dewar and I were at that conference in Kingston all day yesterday," Mel said, defensively. "You know, the Pan-Caribbean Literary Congress. Mr. Dewar was speaking at the dinner in the evening. We were very late back, and there was no light on in Mrs. Dewar's room. We thought she must be asleep. Even this morning, when Mr. Dewar looked in and found the bed hadn't been slept in, we never

15

suspected there was anything wrong. We thought she must have decided to stay here at the beach house."

It sounded terribly thin, but it was the truth. It was equally true that a few hours free from Felicity Dewar was a precious relief.

"That would have been a bit way out, even for Felicity," Lisa remarked, and there was a quality in her tone which jarred on Mel's ears. She glanced quickly at her, but the honey-brown face revealed nothing.

"Then, a bit later, Mr. Dewar decided that he must have his watch—it was at a jewellery store in Kingston being repaired—and he remembered that Mrs. Dewar had an appointment with the doctor this morning. He told me to phone a message through to her, to pick up the watch for him on her way home."

An expression of blank disbelief spread over Lisa's face.

"He'd a hope! Since when did Felicity run errands for *anyone*?"

Mel recognised a truth when she heard it: the dead woman would not have gone to the corner of the street for God Almighty.

"In any case, she wasn't at the consulting rooms," she said uncomfortably, wondering if Dominic was an incurable optimist or plain devious. "She hadn't shown up."

That was the moment when she sensed impending disaster. Felicity looked the picture of health but she had been insistent that she needed to see the doctor. It was inconceivable that she had forgotten the appointment.

"So then I phoned the hairdresser. She was supposed to go there before meeting the doctor. To deal with all those dark roots she had discovered," Mel added wryly, recalling the fuss which Felicity had kicked up when she perceived

16

that her long blonde hair was betraying its origins. "She would have kept that appointment if she had had to be carried in, feet first."

As she spoke, two boats rounded the headland. The first was a white-hulled dinghy with an outboard motor which Mel recognised instantly. Behind it came a launch, manned by a uniformed crew, the green, black and gold of the Jamaican flag fluttering in the wind.

"There go Dominic and the police," said Lisa, unnecessarily.

No sooner had the sound of the boats died away than there was a car jolting up the rough track which served the beach house as a drive. More police, a sergeant and a couple of constables, very polite, very formal, come to take statements, and, it seemed, to keep some sort of watch. Mel had only vague notions of police procedure at home in England, and no knowledge of what went on here, but it looked as though the entire police force of Port Antonio were concentrated on Felicity. Perhaps they had nothing else to do, or, more likely, it was in deference to Justin French. He was the sort of man to expect—and receive—V.I.P. treatment.

Justin himself returned to the beach house before the sergeant had finished taking her statement, bringing with him his cousin and Tib Morley. Mel found herself banished to the verandah, while the men talked with the police, and the light faded rapidly. The darkness was loud with the song of crickets, while moths fluttered round the lights, and tiny, pink-bellied, patient lizards waited for them to come within range of their long sticky tongues. Lisa was with her, but conversation did not flourish.

Mel had her own problems: the arrival of the police had

17

taken her unawares. She had not given a thought to the formalities attendant on sudden death. When the sergeant had asked her name, without thinking, she had announced herself as Melissa Grainger, the part she was playing to all the world. Only when he wrote it down and began taking her statement, did it occur to her that she might be committing some sort of crime, but by then it was already too late to backtrack and admit that she was Melinda. The thought of the subsequent explanations not only to the police, but to Justin and his family were too mind-boggling. She determined that the real Melissa would be back in her own shoes at the first possible moment.

Then the doors of the lounge opened, and Dominic walked onto the verandah.

"Come on, Mel," he said, "I'll take you home."

It was arranged that Justin would ride back with the Morleys, whose car was in Port Antonio, while Dominic took his cousin's car. Relief flooded through Mel: a private word with her employer was her first priority, with the hotel in Kingston where Melissa was staying coming a close second.

It seemed that Dominic was equally anxious.

"You didn't tell the police who you are," he said, as they drove away from the beach house.

"No. It didn't occur to me, until I realised that they wanted a statement, and it was too late then. Mrs. Morley was there, too."

Although it was dark and she could not see his face, she sensed a relaxation of tension.

"Good girl! It would be very damn difficult to explain what you are doing here."

"But I'm going to have to sign that statement. The

18

sergeant said it would be brought to Kingston later tonight."

"Then Melissa can sign it herself. If you don't mind, we'll drive straight over and pick her up."

"Mind?" squeaked Mel, feeling like the relieved defenders of Mafeking. "Mind? I must have been off my head ever to have taken on this substitution."

"Oh, I don't know," Dominic replied easily. "It worked, didn't it?"

"Yes, I suppose so, but with Mrs. Dewar being killed, it all seems so cheap."

"You're right there," he agreed. "Anyway, it will all be over soon. Melissa can ride back home with me and no one need ever know."

It was a frightening drive, over the tortuous mountain road, in the intense darkness, for it was too early for the benefit of moonlight, but Mel would have braved worse than that to extricate herself from involvement with Dominic Dewar. It came to her that she had seen the last of his cousin. That was a relief, too, for Justin French bothered her, why she could not imagine. She had deceived him successfully, along with the other members of his household, yet none of them aroused in her such a feeling of doom.

Melissa was hidden in a quiet hotel at Constant Spring, on the outskirts of Kingston. She had a self-catering cottage and instructions to keep clear of the public rooms of the hotel, and to stay within the grounds, lest she might be seen and recognised, remote though that possibility might be. The twins had spent a few hours together there, on Melinda's arrival from England, checking their appearances, making sure Melinda's tan, which came out of a bottle, corresponded to the natural shade acquired by Melissa, and the necessary briefing. Melinda's own luggage and passport were left there, in her sister's keeping.

The cottage lay at the far side of the hotel garden, near the swimming pool. It was one of a group of four, shaded by an immense mango tree. There were lights in three of the cottages, but the fourth—Melissa's—was in darkness.

Dominic swore.

"Where the devil can she be?"

They pounded on the door, thinking that she might have fallen asleep, but obtained no reply. Then Dominic strode off to look for her in the public rooms of the hotel, for Melissa was not one to obey instructions if the mood took her. Mel waited by the cottage, filled with a growing conviction that Melissa had let her down.

A woman came out of the cottage next door, and stopped short when she saw Mel.

"Looking for someone?" she inquired suspiciously, in a sharp American voice.

Mel's heart sank. This was Melissa's neighbour, who should, by rights, take her for her twin. Instead, she was looking on her as an intruder, maybe even a burglar. Clearly, she had never laid eyes on Melissa.

"My sister, but she doesn't seem to be here," she said hastily.

"Why, you must be English!" came the surprised reply, but in a more friendly tone. "I'd know that cute accent anywhere. Your sister, you say? Is she supposed to be in next door?"

"Yes. She was here a couple of days ago."

"She's not here now. We moved in yesterday, and the maid told me that place is empty. I guess your sister took off. Maybe she left a note for you with the desk clerk."

"Yes, perhaps she has. My friend has gone to inquire. Thank you," Mel stammered, wondering what Melissa was playing at. She did not doubt for a moment that the woman was speaking the truth. Melissa was not here.

Dominic returned, looking furious.

"We are wasting our time," he said shortly. "Get in the car. We might as well go home."

Mel had no desire to discuss the position in front of strangers, and the American woman was hovering in the doorway of her cottage. She took her place beside Dominic.

"Where is she?" she demanded, as they drove away.

"God knows! She has gone for a cruise with that boy friend of hers. She told the clerk to hold her room, and said she would be back sometime tomorrow."

That would be December the twenty-third, the last day of the deception. They would be flying off for their holiday in the Virgin Islands the next morning. Melissa had it all worked out.

"I'm sorry, Mel," Dominic was saying. "I had no idea she was going to do this. She was supposed to be at hand in case you ran into trouble, so that we could switch back immediately. She must have been very damn sure that you could take her place and no one would notice."

Mel sighed.

"She knew I could. We have done it hundreds of times. And nobody has rumbled me, have they?"

"No. But it is hardly the point. Just when we want her, she is not here."

For Mel, it was a moment of enlightenment, as she recalled certain things about her twin sister which had slipped from her mind during the years of estrangement. Melissa would not have changed, for all that she was eager to re-

21

establish contact.

"I should have known," she said, at last.

"Known what?" Dominic demanded.

"That Melissa had her own private reasons for setting up this substitution trick. I expect you think it was all your idea, but, for my money, she put it into your head. How long have you known that she had a twin?"

"Only a couple of months," he said, uneasily. "What do you mean, her own private reasons?"

"Melissa is very devious, and she is a bit wild, too. It's my guess that she wanted to wangle an extra holiday to spend with this boy friend. Who is he?"

"Jim Something-or-other. Brown, I think. That's right. Jim Brown. He has a boat, and she has been aching to go out in it."

"Did she ask for time off to go with him?

"Yes, she did," Dominic growled. "Now I come to think of it, it must have been just before we started talking about this twin thing. The little devil! She was getting back at me for not letting her go."

"Why didn't you? Can't secretaries take time off when they want?" Mel inquired, slightly nettled at the tone she detected in his voice.

Dominic sighed.

"That was Felicity's doing," he said, the anger gone, leaving only dejection. "She was keen for me to finish my new book. She wouldn't hear of Mel taking time off. Oh, well, none of it matters now."

"It does to me!" Mel retorted. "The police know me as Melissa Grainger. What do I do now?"

"Can't you carry on? It is only until tomorrow night. She will be back by then."

22

Dubiously, Mel agreed. There seemed no harm in it. She had only herself to blame. She should have known better than involve herself in one of Melissa's schemes.

There seemed little point in revealing the truth. It would provoke a dreadful row in the family, and might even lose Melissa her job, though that was all she deserved for manoeuvring her sister and her employer into this position. But she could not have known that Felicity would meet with a fatal accident, and it would be Dominic who would have to bear the odium. He had trouble enough. The least she could do was help him through until her wayward sister reappeared.

They were running through the lighted streets of Kingston now. The stores were still open, thronged with Christmas shoppers. Windows displayed winter scenes, with sledges and cotton wool snow, for a population which, except for those who had travelled and the visitors, had never seen the real thing. In the hot night, Father Christmasses sweated in robes and beards. Mel thought swiftly of home and the empty house she had left behind, the cold Christmas to which she had thought herself condemned. It occurred to her that, now that the first shock of Felicity's death was wearing off, she was not really sorry she had come.

They left the town behind, climbing into the hills again, up the dark twisting road which led to Eagles' Nest, Justin French's palatial home. Below them lay the sprawl of lights which was Kingston, and beyond that, the long spit of land of the Palisadoes, with the brilliance of the airport and the glint of the sea under the night sky.

The gates of Eagles' Nest loomed up in front of them, standing wide, but with a uniformed policeman checking all arrivals. Outside the house were parked several cars, some with police markings. As Dominic pulled up, someone came to the open front door, and out onto the steps. The light from inside showed it to be Justin French.

"Dominic! Where the devil have you been?" he demanded, striding over to the car.

"Taking my time," his cousin returned calmly. "Was there a hurry?"

Justin made a gesture of impatience.

"It doesn't matter, now that you are here. The police are waiting for you."

"Who is it? Anyone we know?"

Justin shook his head.

"Minions only, at the moment. A C.I.D. sergeant. The top brass will be here later, I don't doubt."

Dominic nodded, and went into the house without another word.

Mel would have followed him, but found her arm held in a detaining grip.

"A word of warning," said Justin, in her ear, and in no encouraging tone. "Don't take the police for fools. Watch your step."

Mel stared at him, but his back was to the lights of the house and his face was in shadow.

"What do you mean? I'm sorry Mrs. Dewar is dead, but it is nothing to do with me. I can't tell the police anything about the accident."

"What accident?" he threw back at her, harshly. "Don't play your games with me, Mel. You know as well as I do that Felicity was murdered."

TWO

"Murdered?" Mel squeaked, as if she had never heard the word before. But it registered all the same, and several things which had been bothering her clicked into place. She cursed herself for a fool: of course it was murder!

Justin replied with a short humourless laugh.

"You did that marvellously. Have you been rehearsing it all the way home?" Through the darkness, she felt his eyes searching her face. "If it's genuine, I shouldn't have interfered," he went on. "The police should have been the ones to hear that note of innocence. I doubt if you will be able to repeat it exactly like that."

Mel pulled herself together, as the frightful implications of his words began to sink in.

"Mr. French, are you insinuating that I had something to do with Mrs. Dewar's death?"

"Did you?" he countered.

"No, I did not!" she replied indignantly.

"Carry on like that and they won't be able to get anywhere near you," Justin said admiringly.

Anger suddenly boiled over in Mel.

"Just what is all this? Why should anyone imagine that I would go around murdering people?"

"Not people in general. Only one person: Felicity Dewar. Come on, Mel! You must have realised that the

25

whole house heard Dominic and Felicity going hammer and tongs the other night. All about you! In any case, I doubt if any of us needed telling that Felicity suspected you of having designs on her husband. Right from the moment you all arrived here, it was obvious that she had her jealous beady eye fixed on the pair of you."

Mel thought furiously of her absent sister: this was part of the essential briefing which had been omitted. Angry though she was with Justin French for his suspicions, her common sense told her that unwittingly, he had done her a favour. It would have been very disconcerting to hear all this for the first time from the police. Now, at least, she could prepare herself.

"I suppose you have told the police all about it?" she inquired crossly.

"They won't hear of it from me," Justin shot back at her, and she detected anger in his voice, too. "However, there are other people living in my house. One of them will be sure to mention it."

"I don't see why you don't go right ahead and tell them yourself!"

His grip on her arm tightened and he gave her a little shake.

"Can't you understand that I want to help you?"

"Why should you?" Mel demanded.

"Because Dominic is more my brother than my cousin. We were brought up together. When we were boys I always looked after him. How do you suppose I felt seeing him eaten alive by that bitch? I know she is dead, but it doesn't alter the fact of what she was. You can't have worked for him for so long without finding out about Felicity. You received your share of the treatment, too, I don't doubt."

26

" You think *he* killed her? How are you so sure that it wasn't an accident, anyway?"

" She was transfixed by that harpoon. It must have been shot at very close range. No one could have done that by accident. The cord attaching it to the gun was severed, not broken. Besides, that was new equipment. I should know. I bought it."

" What?"

" That fish spear came from the beach house. One is missing from there, and the one that killed her bears my markings. So it is murder, and close to home. The husband is the obvious suspect," he went on, his voice harsh with suppressed anger. "What else are the police expected to think? A rich woman is killed, and there is a history of quarrels over the husband's secretary."

" Whatever Mrs. Dewar imagined, there was no foundation for it," Mel told him, convinced she could speak not only for herself but for Melissa, too. She had perceived no attachment between her sister and Dominic, and she was sure that she would have known. Such things were part of the sympathy which existed between them as identical twins.

" I would like to believe that," said Justin unexpectedly. " The thing that worries me is what you have been up to these past few days."

Mel received a severe jolt. She knew better than he did what his words meant: Justin could perceive a difference between her and Melissa, although, since he did not know of the existence of a twin, he could explain it only in terms of 'being up to something'. Apart from their parents, no one, before this moment, had ever been able to distinguish between them.

" Nothing that concerned Mrs. Dewar," she said, recover-

27

ing swiftly.

"I told you I wanted to help. Not only Dominic, but you, Mel. You can trust me."

She fought down an impulse to confide in him. Shock and something akin to fear were undermining her nerves. He looked like a rock, and the pressure of his fingers on her arm, although it was not meant to be comforting, filled her with an illogical sense of security. She reminded herself that he was virtually a stranger, an unknown quantity.

"Thank you," she murmured, making an effort to steady herself. "You are very kind, Mr. French."

"Kind? That is not my general reputation! But I wish you no harm, Mel. Felicity was bad news when she was alive and now she is dead she can still do terrible damage."

The ferocity in his voice startled Mel.

"She has been murdered! Whatever she did in life, that makes her a victim, too."

"Thanks for reminding me," he snapped back.

Mel could have kicked herself for her clumsiness. She was in no position to look a gift horse in the mouth, and Justin was offering to lend support if the need arose.

"I'm sorry," she said. "I wasn't trying to rebuke you. None of this is my affair!"

"Good God, girl! How many times do you have to be told? Even if Felicity hadn't been laying down poison about you to anyone who would listen, you, as her husband's secretary, would be bound to come in for your share of suspicion. You are ten years younger that she was, you are good-looking and you enjoy life. She wasn't wearing well. She had been around too much. She had three broken marriages behind her, and the fourth one was drifting onto the rocks. No one," he went on in a tone of unaccountable

28

bitterness," could blame Dominic if he—"

"Well, he didn't!" Mel broke in, heatedly. "How many times do *you* have to be told? I hope the police will not be equally obtuse. In any case, I do not see how they can entertain suspicions of either Mr. Dewar or myself, no matter how much gossip they hear. Mrs. Dewar did not come home last night, so presumably she was killed at some time during the day?"

"Possibly. Even probably. We shall know soon enough. You have a good clear head on your shoulders, Mel, I'll give you that. The body was stiff when we found her. I'm not familiar with the technicalities of rigor, but I think she must have been dead many hours."

"It must have been done in daytime, or she would hardly have been wearing a bikini," Mel pointed out. "So yesterday is the day, and that lets out both Mr. Dewar and myself. We spent the entire day at the conference in Kingston, in the company of a hundred other people. Neither of us could have driven over to the beach house at any time," she added, and suddenly wondered why Justin had professed such concern for herself and Dominic. He knew perfectly well where they had been all day. So why the fears for his cousin? A suspicion crept into her mind: perhaps Justin was not being entirely frank when he said that he wanted to help. She shuddered at how close she had been to confessing to him the truth about herself.

"Assassins can be hired," he said. "Especially when one has a thundering good alibi."

Mel stared at him, appalled, biting back a sharp rejoinder. The dreadful part was that he was right: she knew so little of Dominic Dewar that she could form no opinion as to whether he would scheme to rid himself of his wife. If he had, then her own position was even more dubious than she had thought. So was that of Melissa. They might both be involved, how deeply she dared not speculate. On the other hand, Dominic might be completely innocent, but no policeman would believe that once he got wind of the substitution of the twins. It would look like a conspiracy between the three of them, with herself and Dominic to set up the alibi, while Melissa either committed or arranged the crime. Only Melissa could keep them all out of prison, by providing her own alibi with this boy friend—and Melissa was off the map for the moment, not due back at the hotel for another twenty-four hours.

Mel faced the fact that she was trapped in her sister's identity. If she did not want to spend Christmas in gaol, she must keep up the pretence. Until Melissa returned, her own freedom, and Dominic's, depended on her acting out her part.

Dearly, she wished to have a frank talk with Dominic Dewar. There were questions, too, to which Justin French might supply some answers.

"Why are you telling me this?" she demanded. "Do you *know* that Mr. Dewar paid someone to kill his wife?"

"Good God! What do you take me for?" he retorted. "All I am trying to do is prepare you for the sort of questions the police may ask. I don't know how well you will stand up to this. A lot of white women get uptight when a black detective starts questioning them. It doesn't do any good and it puts their backs up right away. So get this into your head: the police here are not dumb Sambos."

"I never supposed that they were! I fail to see why race should enter into this."

Justin let out a crack of surprised laughter.

" That's refreshing! I wish you could pass on a bit of your common sense to the other females in this house. They seem to think that I should be able to pull strings to prevent them being bothered by a lot of black policemen."

" And can you?"

" I am not going to jeopardise my reputation by trying," he said shortly. " The law has to take its course. However, that doesn't mean that I won't take out a little insurance. Tib Morley is here. He is not only a friend, but the best lawyer in Jamaica. If the going gets sticky with the police, clam up and send for Tib. Come on, now," he said, swinging her round to face the house. " It's time we went in."

Mel permitted him to lead her, for with her arm still in his strong grasp, she had no choice. They went past a bored policeman standing at the door, and into the house.

Eagles' Nest was a long two storey building, an interesting place of split levels as the architect had taken advantage of the natural contours of the hill, spacious, unobtrusively luxurious. Dominic had told her that it was built for Justin's parents, thirty years before, and now their son, a bachelor, lived there alone.

" Except when the family descends upon him," he had added, with a grin," which is all too often to please Justin. Not only is he lumbered with us, at the moment, but he has his step-mother here while her new house is being finished and she has her niece in tow, as well as her son. The house is full."

Mel thought that an overstatement, for Eagles' Nest was very large. She and the Dewars were housed in a guest cottage, separate from the main building, so that only the others were in the house itself.

" Everyone is in the lounge," said Justin, in her ear, and

fleetingly, she wished that she did not have to face these people, all of whom would be thinking that she and her employer were lovers. It was shaming, all the more so, oddly, because it was untrue.

They walked in on a group sitting in uncomfortable silence. Vera French, Justin's step-mother, and her niece, Gina Rawlings, occupied the two ends of a long settee. Both were blondes, and very careful of their appearance, but there the likeness between them ended. Vera was tall and thin, in her early forties, and wore a perpetually worried expression. From time to time, she glanced anxiously towards her son, Aubrey, a youth of sixteen who was sulking in a corner of the vast room. Her niece was in complete contrast. Gina was not much past twenty, but displayed none of the uncertainty of youth. She was petite, like a piece of delicate porcelain, and had the gift of making all other women feel like great hulking lumps. She oozed self-confidence. No one would ever get the better of her, if she could help it.

Both women looked up as Justin led Mel into the room. Vera's interest flagged immediately, but Gina followed their progress. Mel recalled that her sister had said that Gina had her eye on Justin.

Facing Vera and Gina, across a low coffee table, but not in conversation with them, were the Morleys. Tib browsed through a newspaper, while Lisa tried to keep from staring at the women, only too well aware that Vera French did not like being in the same room as she, much less being obliged to accept one of her colour as an equal.

Justin thrust Mel into a chair beside Lisa.

"I'll get you a drink," he said, and made for the sideboard, where there were decanters and glasses.

Gina was there before him. It had displeased her to see Justin holding Mel's arm, even though his grip did not suggest any form of tenderness. She did not fear competition, for she considered that largish girls with brown hair were hardly in the same class as petite blondes, but neither did she intend to permit any other female to monopolise the attention of the man she was determined to marry. Now she fussed with the glasses, serving him as well as pouring for Mel, finding means to detain him if only for a moment.

" Gina never gives up," Lisa murmured, so that no one else could hear. " But she is wasting her time. Justin hardly notices her. Fortunately. She is not the girl for him." She paused, to favour Mel with a speculative look, then went on, " You know, it would make more sense if it were Justin who had been killed, not Felicity."

Mel felt her heart leap up into her throat.

" What?" she gasped.

" He has enemies enough. He stands for a future that most of us are not large-minded enough to comprehend. He doesn't give a damn about the colour of a man's skin, while most political issues revolve round it. So there are whites who regard him as a renegade, but he is too important a person to ignore. And there are those of my own people who hate him for the same reason upside down, because he won't conform to the image of the whites that gives them power over the ignorant."

" He has friends, too."

Lisa smiled faintly.

" Oh, yes, but it is enemies who do the killing. That's why I don't understand why Felicity has been murdered. Oh, I grant you she wasn't my favourite person, or yours, either, I guess. If we are honest, we must both admit that neither of us liked her very much. I have heard her bitch at you, and you can't have missed her attitude to me. Like those two," she went on, glancing across at Vera and then at Gina, who was still keeping Justin talking by the sideboard," she thought I was one of a lesser breed, some sort of animal, partially house-trained. I admit that I did not like her, but there is a great gulf between not liking, and hating enough to kill."

Tib Morley had caught his wife's words. He stood up, and came to place himself in front of them so that they formed a little private triangle.

"Hate is not the only motive for murder," he said. "There is also gain—of one sort or another."

"Is there more than one?" Lisa asked.

"Oh, yes. When a rich woman like Felicity dies, one is bound to ask who inherits her money. But there is at least one other possible gain from the death of a wife: the husband's freedom."

Dominic, thought Mel. He might benefit on both counts. Justin had said Felicity was eating him alive, whatever that might mean. It did not sound like the perfect marriage.

Lisa stared up at Tib.

"I don't think I like the idea of that."

Justin came over, playing the good host, bearing a whole tray of glasses, with Gina tagging along. She had a proprietorial air: already in her mind's eye, she was mistress of Eagles' Nest. She spoke polite phrases to Lisa and Tib, but there was no warmth in her for them: her eagerness for Justin and all things his did not extend to his coloured friends.

Their arrival put an end to the uncomfortable conversation between the Morleys and Mel, which to her was a measure of relief, for every word increased her apprehension over her forthcoming interview with the police. Justin and Tib started a discussion over some point of local politics, which she could not follow. Gina and Lisa listened to them, while Vera sat huddled in the corner of the big settee and stared broodingly into space. Aubrey, her son, remained apart, gazing out into the dark garden, with nothing else to relieve his boredom. No one took any notice of Mel, except that from time to time she had the feeling that someone was looking at her, and on each occasion, she glanced up to find Justin's gaze resting on her.

Half an hour dragged past, and then Dominic appeared at the double doors which led to the hall. Behind him came one of the policemen. Immediately, all conversation died. Dominic looked harassed, his hair rumpled as if he had been dragging his fingers through it.

The policeman called out: " Miss Grainger, please."

Mel's heart sank. This was it!

She passed Dominic in the doorway, but with all eyes on them and the policeman close by, there was no opportunity to exchange a word.

She was conducted to Justin's study, which he had handed over to the police for their use. It was at the other side of the hall, down a few shallow steps, as the ground dipped away from the main part of the building, a large airy room with a wall of window from which, by day, there was a breath-taking view of Kingston, several hundred feet below. Now, after dark, the town lay like a carpet of lights.

She was interrogated by a very polite, quietly-spoken sergeant, while a constable laboriously took down every word. In the long intervals of waiting for his pen to catch up, Mel had time to examine the room. It was a masculine place, plain and uncluttered, the walls lined with books. There were a few framed photographs : of one or two school sports teams, and a group in tennis whites; of Dominic, looking young and defenceless; of a woman who must be Justin's mother; of a wedding group in which she recognised Vera, Justin's step-mother, and the elderly man at her side was surely his father. She wondered why Justin had never married, and immediately thought of Gina's ambitions. It was no business of hers, but she caught herself hoping that Gina would not succeed.

The interview was very formal, limited to going over the statement she had made at the beach house, and Mel told herself that she had been an idiot to be so afraid. Her new-found confidence was shaken a little when she was invited to give them her finger-prints, and informed that the Superintendent would be arriving shortly, but she had overcome her initial fears well enough by that time. She comforted herself with the thought that her lies were confined solely to her identity. On all other matters she was telling the truth as she knew it, and that was all the police could desire. She returned to the lounge with a quieter mind than when she had left it.

In her absence, tempers had flared. Now, Aubrey stood in the middle of the large room, confronting his half-brother. He was slim and on the short side, fair like his mother, with none of the French family heritage in evidence. He wore jeans and a tee-shirt, while on his feet were sandals with thick platforms. His face flushed with anger, he looked younger than his sixteen years.

" That old cow's death has nothing to do with me," he stormed. " It's not my scene, man."

Justin lessened the distance between them with two long

strides.

"That's for your foul mouth," he said, and struck him in the face. Aubrey reeled back, while Vera let out a piercing scream and rushed to her son's side.

"You will speak of the dead with respect," Justin said heavily. "And you will remain here, as we all will, until the police have completed their interviews."

Aubrey shook off his mother's clinging hands.

"My friends are waiting for me," he grumbled.

"Then they will have to wait," Justin replied grimly.

"You're going out with that no-good Manley," Vera wailed. "Don't lie to me!"

Aubrey flung her a contemptuous look.

"Cool it, Mom! Since when was that news?"

"Lowering yourself!" Vera went on. "You think more of that black layabout than you do of me."

The colour flamed again in Aubrey's face.

"Manley's not a layabout! He's—"

"That's enough!" Justin roared, and his half-brother subsided. "You can fight over Manley in private, later. For the moment—"

"You don't care what company your brother keeps," Vera interrupted. "Why don't you forbid Aubrey to see Manley? It's your duty now that his father is dead."

"I hope I have more sense!" Justin retorted. "Aubrey is old enough to make his own friends. He is less likely to come to harm through Manley than through some of his fancy school friends," he added, with a meaning stare at his step-mother.

Vera stared back, outraged.

"Justin! There's no need to go into all that!"

"Quite!" he returned coldly. "Now, as I was saying,

for the moment we all have to hold ourselves in readiness for police questioning. However, there is no reason why we should not use the time in trying to sort out a few things for ourselves."

Dominic looked up. He was slumped in a chair set apart from the rest, and had taken no interest in the flair-up with Aubrey.

"What things, for Pete's sake?" he asked, then subsided into his own private world before he had an answer.

"About the circumstances of Felicity's death," Justin told him. "There has to be some connection with us—with this house. We might save ourselves a lot of grief by pooling our knowledge. That is why Tib is here. I've retained his professional services."

"Oh, my God! No!" Vera exclaimed. "Isn't it enough that we have one lot of blacks crawling all over us without bringing in another? Anyway, what is the point? *I* know why Felicity is dead, and so do all of you, but you are too stuck up to admit it." She looked into face after face. "I'm the only one who has the sense to be frightened."

"Now, Vera," said Justin wearily. "Don't start all that nonsense again."

"It's not nonsense," she flared. "It's all very well for you. No one scattered grave dirt in *your* bed."

Mel, who had been hovering near the door, hoping for a chance to slip into some unnoticed chair, felt a chill run down her spine. *What was grave dirt?*

Gina, watching Justin's face carefully, decided it was time for her to act. She jumped up and went to put her arm round Vera.

"Come on, Auntie Vee," she smiled. "That's only a bit of old superstition. Don't get yourself into a state over

38

nothing."

Vera shook off her hand.

"Nothing! You little fool! You are too full of yourself to take heed of a warning when it is given. Grave dirt was put under the pillow of every woman in this house. Yours. Mine. Mel's. And Felicity's. All four of us. It means that someone is trying to kill us. And don't tell me that just because it is illegal that Obeah doesn't exist. It does and it is powerful, or Felicity would be alive this moment. But she isn't. She's dead. As the three of us will be, if we don't get that spell taken off us."

THREE

There was a moment's appalled silence, while Vera gazed round the room in defiant triumph. No one could doubt that she believed every word of it herself: the note of terror was unmistakable. Gina stared at her aunt thoughtfully. Justin looked taken aback, and even Dominic was roused from his withdrawn state. Mel shivered in the warm tropical night, and groped for a chair since her knees refused to support her further. Tib Morley watched them all, the interested spectator, but Lisa, his wife, sensitive to the fear which hung over the room, sat with clenched hands.

Then Dominic shook himself like a man throwing off a drugged sleep.

" The spirits must be losing their grip," he said, " If they are reduced to using human agencies wielding harpoons."

Vera swung round.

" Trust you to mock!"

" Dominic is right," Justin intervened. " Felicity wasn't killed by spirit magic. Obeah has been banned for years. I suppose it is still practised in the country parts, but not here. In any case, we don't know that it was grave dirt that was scattered on the beds last week. It could have been ordinary soil."

" It sent the maids into hysterics. And who would bother

40

to put garden dirt in the bed?"

Mel, ignored on the edge of the group, did not care for the sound of the grave dirt. She had heard talk of Obeah, and knew it was the spirit magic of the island. The thought of it being practised in this house called up primeval fears which, as a modern young woman, she did not know she possessed. The sudden intrusion into her life of ancient beastly rites gave her a taste of the horrors. Melissa had not mentioned it, so if her sister was afraid, she had kept it to herself.

Gina took her cue from Justin, as was her fashion.

"The spirits can't hurt you, Auntie Vee, unless you believe that they have the power. Let the servants think what they choose. Scratch any one of them and you find a superstitious heathen. You don't want to class yourself with them, do you?"

Mel had to give her credit for it: there was no argument which was likely to be more telling with Vera French.

"I gather that you aren't scared by the spirits, Miss Rawlings?" Tib observed.

Gina flashed a glance at him.

"That's right," she said, and turned back to her aunt. "Come on, Auntie Vee!"

Vera, overborne but not convinced, permitted her niece to lead her back to the settee. She sat down in one corner, biting her thumb, and looking round for sympathy. The obvious source of it, her only child, had retired to his chair by the window, entirely unconcerned with his mother's fears.

The butler appeared, a plump elderly man, whose round black face was set tonight in lines of intense disapproval, which not even the oddity of a defective eye could disguise.

" Supper is laid out in the dining-room, sir," he told Justin.

" Thanks, George. We will serve ourselves. Have the police finished with the staff?"

The disapproval on George's face deepened.

" They are in the kitchen now, sir. Will that be all, sir?"

" Yes, thank you, George," Justin replied, then said to the party in general. " Come on, let's eat."

Vera shuddered.

" How can anyone eat?"

" Don't be silly," Justin shot back at her. " I'm hungry if you are not."

Mel was astonished to discover that at the mention of food, she was suddenly ravenous. She glanced at her watch and was surprised at the lateness of the hour.

Justin shepherded them into the dining-room for one of the most bizarre meals of her life. There was one chair too many round the polished table. Clearly, the murder of a member of the family had upset the domestic staff, and somebody could not count. No one chose to sit in Felicity's usual place, at Justin's right hand, so the chair was left unoccupied, like a ritual reminder of the transcience of human life at an antique feast. It was all too effective at Eagles' Nest that night, blunting the keenest appetite. After a while, Justin removed it, but nothing could blot out the impression it evoked: Felicity was an almost tangible presence in the room. Mel was thankful when they returned to the lounge, where George was waiting to serve coffee.

The passage of hours had not lessened her discomfort. She was in this house under false pretences, a stranger, and intruder now that it was a house of bereavement. Longing for the moment when she could slide away to her bedroom, she selected a chair apart from the rest, where, she hoped, she might remain unnoticed. She started towards it, only to find a hand on her arm, drawing her to one of the long settees in the centre of the room.

"Come and sit with me," invited Lisa Morley.

Mel could hardly refuse. It occurred to her that Lisa also was feeling unwanted. She was not family, and to at least two of her companions, was unwelcome for the colour of her skin. During supper, Mel had had plenty of opportunity to watch Vera and her niece. Neither one had addressed so much as one word to either of the Morleys. Nor did they trouble themselves with her own welfare, Mel had noted, but that was customary. Melissa had warned her that Vera thought it disgraceful that the hired help should eat with her employer and his family.

No one paid them any attention. Justin was deep in conversation with Tib at the other side of the room. Vera and Gina sat together on the other settee. Dominic kept apart, lost in grief, or, at least, thought. Aubrey, impervious alike to his mother's terrors and to the fact of sudden death, wandered restlessly about, wishing to escape but held back by his reluctant awe of his half-brother.

"I wonder," said Lisa quietly," who set up that trick with Felicity's chair in the dining-room?"

Mel looked up sharply.

"Set it up? Deliberately?"

"What else? Justin's servants are too well trained to make a mistake like that."

"But why? What is the point?"

Lisa sighed.

"Don't ask me! Perhaps someone wanted to keep us all on edge. You could have cut the atmosphere in there with

43

a knife. Or maybe you don't notice these things."

" I do," Mel acknowledged. She was beginning to think that the paradise of Eagles' Nest had more than its fair share of serpents. One of them knew how to play on the victims' nerves. " I've had just about as much as I can take for today, but I suppose we have to wait for the police to finish."

She remembered that less than a week ago, she had been all excitement, impatient for the college term to end so that she could be free to cross the Atlantic into hot sunshine and the company of all the family which was left to her. Now she would give anything to be back home, even though the house would be cold, and a lonely Christmas colder still.

Justin and Tib Morley had finished their conference. Now they came to the middle of the lounge.

" Tib is going to ask us all some questions," Justin announced. " If we pool our knowledge, perhaps we may contribute towards a quick solution of this crime. It will be in our interest to do so," he added grimly, his eyes on his step-mother. " The police will not let us alone until they are satisfied." He paused to see if anyone wished to raise objections, but Vera contented herself with throwing him a resentful look which Justin took to mean acquiescence. " Carry on, Tib."

The lawyer pulled a chair into a position from which he could see each face, and lowered his large bulk into it. He looked as alert as if it were just the beginning of the day.

" Lisa will take notes for me," he said, and she opened her handbag to bring out a pad and pencil. " Now, briefly, let us see what are the facts. Felicity left this house yesterday

44

morning sometime shortly after eight o'clock, to go to the beach house. She was going alone, and she took with her a packed lunch. She was expected back in the evening. Everyone agreed on that?"

No one spoke.

"Right," Tib continued. "That brings us to the first important question : was she in the habit of going off to the beach house on her own?"

There was a short silence while, it seemed to Mel, everyone waited for the others to speak.

"Someone must know how she spent her time," Tib pointed out. "Dominic?"

The bereaved husband ran his hand through his hair, a favourite gesture when he was puzzled or troubled.

"I don't know what she did with herself while I was working. She was keen for me to get on with this new book. She insisted that I worked regular hours. I didn't inquire how she amused herself."

"I think we can say that she went to the beach house quite a bit," Justin said. "The servants can tell you how often she took a picnic basket. We always do, for the beach house. You know that. There are no supplies available there."

"It's a long drive, for a day on your own."

"The beach is good there, and it is quiet. She found the beaches round here too crowded."

"You mean, she was too stuck up to mingle with people," Vera broke in. "I offered to go with her, to keep her company, once. Never again! Not after that sort of brush-off."

"So," said Tib, "Felicity was in the habit of going to the beach house, and she preferred to be alone. To return to

45

yesterday morning. It was the final day of a conference in Kingston attended by writers from all over the Caribbean. Dominic was one of the speakers. One would have expected Felicity to go with him. Why didn't she?"

" I thought she was. I couldn't believe it when she announced she wasn't going with me," Dominic sighed. " She sprang it on me at breakfast time. She used to like that sort of thing, queening it as the wife of a prize-winning author. Except that my last two books have been flops," he added bitterly. " Maybe that is why she wouldn't go."

Tib looked across at Mel.

" Did she tell you why she had decided not to go to the conference?"

" I was there when she told Mr. Dewar," Mel replied uncomfortably. " But to me it sounded more like an excuse than a real reason. She just didn't want to go."

" What was the excuse?"

" She said she wasn't going to show herself in public until she had been to the hairdresser. She wasn't a natural blonde and the day before she had discovered that the dark roots were showing. She blamed the climate here, making her hair grow quicker than usual."

" And who, apart from you, Dominic, and Miss Grainger, here, knew that Felicity had changed her mind about attending the conference, and was going, instead, to the beach house?" Tib asked of the company at large.

" I knew," Justin volunteered. " Dominic called me at the office."

Vera and Gina looked at each other uncertainly.

" Oh, cripes! We all knew," Aubrey put in, indicating for the first time that he was following the proceedings. " Even I did, and I didn't care how Felicity passed her time. That old cat couldn't get by without having the attention of the entire household. I heard her going on to you, Mom, and Gina, about how slow the cook was in packing that lunch basket."

"And, of course, the servants would know," Tib suggested, and Justin nodded curtly.

"The staff have worked here for years, most of them," he said unhappily. "I can't see any one of them being a murderer, or a murderer's accomplice."

A faint smile touched Tib's mouth.

"No doubt they would be grateful for the testimonial, Justin, but we can't leave anyone out. They, or any of you, might have passed on information without knowing how it would be used. Does any of you recall mentioning this to an outsider?"

There was a dead silence.

"Let us go a little further," Tib went on, and Mel was aware of a strange impression that at least one person present was relieved at the change of subject. Exchanging thoughts, all her life, with her twin had developed a certain facility in telepathy and she knew she was tuned in to one of them, but who, she had no notion. Yet she was sure that someone breathed more freely.

"So far," Tib was saying, "all that we have established is that quite a number of persons knew where Felicity was going. She reached the beach house and changed into her bathing suit. This is where we move into unknown territory. We don't know when she was killed."

"Her picnic basket hadn't been touched," Justin put in. "It was in the beach house."

"Which suggests that she was killed during the morning," Tib commented. "But it is not conclusive evidence.

47

Neither do we know where she was killed. It could have been at the house, at sea, or at the place where she was found, or, indeed, anywhere else. If it was at the house, there are bound to be traces. The one thing we do know about her death is that the murder weapon came from the beach house. Are you sure about that, Justin?"

"Quite sure. The markings on it are clear. And there is a spear missing."

"Only the harpoon? What about the gun which fires it?"

"That is there. I saw it."

"I don't understand," Vera interrupted, petulantly. "What difference does it make?"

"Only that it means one of us did it," Aubrey told her. "Any fool should be able to see where Tib is heading. If Felicity was killed at the beach house, there is an outside possibility that a stranger did it, while he was robbing the place. If she wasn't, it means that someone took the gun and the spear from the beach house, and put the gun back when they had finished with it. It also means that Felicity must have let them into the house, and gone out in a boat with them. Can you see her doing that for a stranger? Fat chance!"

"That is remarkably well put," said Tib. "Thank you, Aubrey."

"I didn't aim to help," replied Aubrey, and resumed his post staring out of the window into the dark garden.

"I will not sit here and listen to my own son accuse his family of murder!" Vera wailed.

"Better to hear it from him than from the police," Justin retorted.

"Auntie Vee, it really is an advantage to know what we

48

are up against," Gina added, eager to gain Justin's approval. "No one can accuse you, anyway. You had your Red Cross meeting in the morning, and you were playing Bridge with Mrs. Whiteman in the afternoon. I'm sure the police will discover that some local from Port Antonio is guilty."

"You can be certain that they will make the most thorough inquiries," Tib pointed out. "I'm grateful to you, Miss Rawlings, for leading into my next point. The police will want to know the movements of all of you during yesterday. We know where Dominic and Miss Grainger were. Now we can account for Mrs. French. Which leaves you, Miss Rawlings, Justin and Aubrey."

"I was shopping in Kingston in the morning, had lunch in town and came back here around half-past two," Gina replied. "I'm afraid it is all very vague. But, you know, I am not your ideal suspect. I had never met Felicity before she came to stay here. We had very little in common and she was a lot older than I. We were virtual strangers."

"Lucky you!" Aubrey exclaimed. "Everyone who knew her loathed her. You, too, Tib, I shouldn't wonder. Felicity was pretty rude to you and Lisa, on account of you being black, and her being an aristocratic Southern Belle. Except, of course, that she wasn't. She came from New Orleans, all right, but her Pa started out as a slum kid without a pair of shoes to his feet."

"Good God! How did you discover that?" demanded Justin, involuntarily.

Aubrey grinned.

"I have my methods! I thought it might be useful to know a bit about where the Farrell bread came from. Felicity's old man worked it all up from zero. Farrell's

Frisky Fella dog-food empire was all his own creation."

" Bully for him!" Dominic commented. " I liked Felicity's father. Though how you managed to find out all that when I have been married to her for four years and have never heard a word about it, I don't know! Did you tell Felicity that you knew?"

Aubrey's grin broadened.

" Oh, yes! She nearly bust a gut. Sorry, Tib, I can't put up much of an alibi for yesterday, but if there was any murdering to be done between me and Felicity, I would have been the victim."

" For the record, what were you doing?" Tib asked, unmoved.

" I was round and about."

" Ask for Manley and no doubt he will be able to tell you where Aubrey was," said Vera, in a brittle voice. " Manley's parents are our butler and our cook, and my son sees fit to spend all his time in that company!"

" Now, Mom—" Aubrey began, but his voice was drowned out.

" That's enough!" Justin roared. " Vera, please do not raise that subject again this evening. And you, Aubrey, don't need to rush to Manley's defence every time his name is mentioned. You forget that both Dominic and I have known him all his life. I'm sorry about that, Tib. This is a perennial family dispute. I think I am the only one who hasn't accounted for his movements yesterday. I was at the office until about nine-thirty, then I was due at the bauxite plant. But even that is not quite straightforward," he added, with a faint smile. " I had a flat tyre on the way, miles from anywhere. The spare wheel was down and I had to walk to a village to borrow a foot pump. By the time I was through,

I was so late that I gave up the trip and came back to Kingston. I might add that I was alone, driving myself. Sorry I can't do any better."

"It will do, for the time being," Tib replied evenly. "One thing more. Felicity was expected back last night. Why wasn't the alarm raised when she didn't show up?"

"I wasn't her keeper," Vera snapped. "It was no business of mine—or Gina's—what Felicity did with herself."

"I was out to dinner," Justin supplied.

"And I was only too damn glad not to have her sour old puss glaring at me across the table to ask why she wasn't there," Aubrey put in, cheerfully, and earned himself another black look from his half-brother.

"I guess it was my fault," Dominic observed. "You all know how it was with Felicity and me. We haven't slept together in the last two years. I didn't look in on her when I came home from the Congress because she wouldn't have thanked me to wake her up to tell her about it. Even in the morning, when I realised she hadn't come home, I didn't think anything of it. She had a fancy man on the north shore. I thought she was with him. It never crossed my mind that there might be anything wrong until we found out that she had skipped her morning appointments."

"So you knew about the boy friend?" Justin exclaimed. "You didn't tell me."

Dominic shrugged weary shoulders.

"I have been trying to stand on my own feet, for a change. I guess you knew, too?"

"I had my suspicions."

"Felicity was as mad as hell when you had a go at her about him," Aubrey broke in. "I know. I heard every gorgeous word."

"Have you taken to listening at keyholes," Justin demanded.

Aubrey flipped a lazy hand.

"Not me, man! The way you two carried on, you could have been heard in Montego Bay. I expect Mom and Gina listened in, but they are too ladylike to admit it."

Vera flushed up, and began a hot denial, but at that moment, there appeared a blaze of headlights as a car swept up the drive, to distract the attention of all. Outside, in the hall, they heard men's voices, and the clatter of official boots. The Top Brass had arrived.

FOUR

The C.I.D. Superintendent turned out to be a slender tallish man, coffee-coloured, dapper in fawn tropical suiting, immaculate white shirt and a bronze striped tie. Mel looked into his sharp brown eyes and her heart sank. She was tired from the happenings of the day, and edgy from the long wait for this inevitable moment. Superintendent Marshall had taken his witnesses in strict priority, starting with the bereaved husband, then the family, and now he had reached the employees. Only the servants would have a longer wait than she, and they, she reflected wryly, had nothing to fear.

Her own position she felt to be next to impossible. She dared not tell the truth. Until Melissa showed up, she must act out her part, but she was filled with the dread that they were being used. Melissa would never have gone blithely off to sea if she had been conspiring with Dominic to murder his wife, for she could not be sure that her twin would keep up the deception to the police. Or could she? Memories crowded in on Mel: Melissa had always assumed that Melinda would back her to the hilt. She thrust the thoughts aside. Whatever Melissa's part, there remained the possibility that Dominic had taken advantage of the substitution of the twins to arrange Felicity's death. Certainly, he had used her to uncover the fact that his wife was missing—that business about fetching the watch was phoney

53

—and as Justin had pointed out, she could make denials of a love affair with her employer ring absolutely true. The whole thing was a mess, but this was not the moment to indulge in speculation. She looked across the desk at the Superintendent and resolved to stick to the facts as she knew them.

It was easier than she anticipated: Marshall confined his questions to a detailed account of her movements and those of Dominic from the moment of leaving Eagles' Nest for the Writers' Congress to the time when they realised that Felicity was missing. She refused to be drawn on the subject of the dead woman's character, and the state of her relations with her husband. Mel was surprised that the Superintendent let her off so lightly, until he warned her, as she was about to leave the room, that he was certain she had a great deal more to tell him—in the near future.

If only you knew, she thought, and fled.

She heard Justin's voice in the hall behind her, but then the Superintendent called him and she was able to make her escape.

The guest cottage was built at right angles to the house itself, a bungalow containing a pair of double bedrooms leading off a lounge, with a small third room—hers—tucked in to one side, the whole shaded by a wide verandah, and set beside the swimming pool. She was relieved to see lights on inside, and hoped that Dominic was alone.

He was on the verandah, his chair pushed back into the shadows so that she did not see him until he rose to meet her.

"Thank God! I thought you would never come. What did Superintendent Marshall ask you?"

"A lot less than I expected, and quite a bit more than

54

I could answer, as it was!" she replied sharply, her resentment against her sister and the whole mad scheme boiling up.

Dominic's shoulders sagged.

"Come in and have a drink," he said wearily. "Mel, I can't tell you how sorry I am that you are stuck with all this!"

She followed him into the lounge, smitten with remorse that she had snapped at him. If her situation was bad, his was infinitely worse.

"I can hang on until Melissa comes back," she said, "but there are things that I have to know. Personal things. I'm sorry to have to pry, especially at a time like this."

He was busy with glasses, his back towards her.

"You want to know if I was having an affair with Melissa, is that it?"

"Partly. Were you?"

"No. You will have to take my word for that."

"I gather that your wife suspected that you were."

"Oh, that? Window-dressing. She had divorce in mind, and was looking round for an excuse. That is why she insisted on bringing Melissa along on this trip. She was hoping the tropical climate would tempt us into some sort of indiscretion that she could use."

"I thought divorce was easy in the United States?" asked Mel, puzzled. "Why didn't she go to Reno?"

"Not Felicity's style, at all, believe me. I was to be the guilty party, just like my three predecessors, poor devils. You knew she was a much-married lady? It was her weakness—marrying men with some claim to fame and not much money. An expensive hobby, since she was prepared to support them while the marriage lasted, but not a penny

55

after that. When she wanted out, she fixed things so that there was no nice financial settlement, just the order of the boot."

"And how did you feel about that?"

She saw his hand tighten on the glass he was holding. With the other he poured spirit and slopped it on the table.

"I wasn't consulted," he said, trying to achieve a light tone and failing. "I'm one of those fools who believe in married people staying together, even if the glamour has worn off. Does this answer your questions, Mel?"

"Not quite," she admitted, reluctantly. "I'm sorry to insist, but I don't want to put my foot in it with the police."

"You have the right. I got you into this. It's just that I don't like baring my soul. What else do you need to know?"

"Whatever a secretary should know about her employer and his wife. Melissa has been with you for two years, living in your house."

"Right on! You don't need to spell it out. Melissa is a very observant person, and I doubt if there is a single little thing about Felicity and me that she doesn't know." He swung round, glasses in hand. "O.K. Potted biography coming up!"

He handed her a drink, which Mel took, wondering how much she had drunk during the dragging hours. More than she was used to, but it seemed to have little effect. Murder was a sobering influence.

Dominic slumped down into a chair, and for a moment the room was silent save for the discreet humming of the air conditioner in one corner.

"I guess you know more about me as a writer than Melissa does," he said unexpectedly. "English is your speciality, isn't it?"

"Yes. As a matter of fact, I'm teaching a Modern Literature course this year. Your book—your prize-winning book," Mel corrected herself hastily, aware that she had all but let out her opinion that Dominic Dewar was a one-book author, "is part of it."

"You don't have to specify which book," he replied with a twisted grin. "There is only one that is worth anything, as you very well know."

Mel felt acutely uncomfortable. She searched for some tactful phrase, but it seemed that Dominic did not require an answer.

"That happens to some writers," he swept on. "One book, and that's the finish, even if they turn out a lifetime of rubbish afterwards. Maybe I'm one of those. If I am, I am not yet ready to admit it. That's why we came here, to go back to where I started, recapture the original inspiration."

"I thought you were American."

"By accident of birth. My father is a United States citizen, and I was born in New York. My mother is Mexican. But if I am anything at all, I am Jamaican. My parents abandoned me when I was four years old. My mother ran away with a Brazillian playboy, and my father didn't give a damn what happened to me. He shipped me over here, to my mother's sister, along with other unwanted personal effects Mama had left behind. So I was brought up here, in this house, and don't get the idea that I wasn't happy. I never missed my parents and I haven't seen either of them in years. When my Aunt Carmelita died, I mourned her as

57

my mother, and the same thing goes for the Old Man, five years ago. I married Felicity not long after Uncle Andrew went. I've often wondered if I was looking for emotional security. Fat chance with Felicity! I didn't take me long to find out why she had married me. It was that damned literary prize. If she had met me the year before, when I was a struggling unknown, she wouldn't have spared me a second glance. But I haven't been able to make the grade. Felicity was interested only in successful people. I was writing a book when we were married, but somehow that never got finished. I've published two since, and both are junk. One more like that and my reputation, such as it is, will be ruined."

Mel was still stuck for words. She had read the few completed chapters of the new book, and formed an unfavourable opinion. Dominic's self-criticism was realistic, but did it stretch to an honest appraisal of this last chance?

"Felicity had it all weighed up," he said, bitterly. "For her there was only one thing to do with failures: ditch them."

"And was she going to do that?"

"Back home in New York I was sure of it. Then we came here, and she suddenly became keen on the new book, insisting that I worked regular hours, and keeping my nose down to it generally. I kidded myself that she cared for me, after all, until I realised what she was doing."

"And what was that?"

"Killing two birds with one stone: throwing Melissa and me together and keeping me out of her way, so that she could go off with that new boy friend she had picked up."

Mel sat up. She had not been thinking straight. The boy friend might take the murder out of the family circle.

"Had she? Are you sure?"

Dominic shook his head.

"Not if you mean, did I have proof? But I knew Felicity to the bottom of her mean little soul. There was a young musician, last year, that she met at some party. They had a thing going for a little while, but it fizzled out. I remember how she was then, and I have seen the same signs here, over the past couple of months. There was a boy friend somewhere. No doubt the police will uncover him."

"He could have killed her."

"It's an attractive thought," Dominic agreed, "but what motive could he have? His interest would be to have her alive. A rich wife isn't easy to find for a young man on his way up from the bottom."

It seemed to Mel that her employer did not have a highly developed sense of self-preservation.

"You could at least let the police know you suspected a boy friend. It might divert their attention from you. From us," she added.

Dominic shook his head.

"They will lose interest in us soon enough. They have to go through the motions."

Mel stared at him in blank astonishment. His words could mean only one thing.

"You *know* who killed her? That Voodoo thing?"

"Good grief, no! It's Obeah anyway, here in Jamaica. How much do you know about Jamaican politics?"

"Not a thing."

"I won't go into details, but there is a wind of change blowing in Jamaica, and there are various groups of people who don't like its direction. There is a lot of unrest, and for months we had a state of emergency. There have been

59

killings."

"But how could Felicity be mixed up in local politics?"

"She wasn't. Not her scene at all. But Justin is an important man. He is rich, influential, and politically active. I know he has received threats, not that he takes any notice of them."

"You think she was killed because she was related to him, and staying in his house?"

"It's the only explanation that holds water. She was warned not to go to the beach house alone, but she wouldn't listen. I guess she thought the boy friend would protect her. God knows what has happened to him. Fed to the barracuda, I shouldn't wonder."

Mel shuddered.

"Then why leave her on the beach?"

"To point up the warning to Justin. The police haven't a hope in hell of finding who did it." He passed his hand over his face. "God, what a waste! To be killed for a cause you know nothing about, never even heard of! Poor Felicity! She always thought she could manipulate everyone and everything to suit herself."

It seemed a fitting epitaph. Although she had hardly known her, Mel had recognised Felicity as one of those over-confident women who arouse in all other females the desire to see them slip on a banana-skin. Poor Felicity indeed. One mistake had cost her her life.

If it were true that the motive was political. Mel could not help but feel that it was all very convenient to put it down to some faceless assassin. And there was the matter of the grave dirt, the very thought of which sent shivers down her spine.

"Mrs. French has an alternative theory," she pointed out.

" She is scared stiff."

" She is, isn't she? Fascinating the way a bit of primitive magic has stripped the veneer right off her," said Dominic in a detached sort of voice. " Now, Gina, who is just as Jamaican as Vera, doesn't give a rap for the spirits. A hard little piece, that one."

" Melissa didn't tell me about the grave dirt."

" I guess she thought nothing of it. She wasn't frightened. Are you?"

" It's nothing to do with me. It wasn't put in my bed. I don't like it, though."

" That's interesting. You and your sister aren't really alike, except in appearance."

" Not the slightest little bit. I'm the cautious type."

" Yet you fell in with her scheme to change places here. That doesn't seem to be in character."

Mel thought that this was hardly the time or the place to discuss her motives. She was not at all sure of them herself.

" Every dog must have his day," she said shortly. " I had just spent a couple of years nursing first one parent and then the other through their last illnesses. I was tired and depressed and I didn't relish spending Christmas on my own. Melissa's letter arrived the day after my father's funeral."

There was more to it than that, but she would scarcely admit even to herself that what she really could not face was meeting Scott and Helen, who were coming home to England on leave from Africa. Her one-time fiancé and her one-time best friend. Much water might have flowed under the bridge, but it was bitter still.

" What about the arrangements for Mrs. Dewar?" she

asked, to draw her employer away from the dangerous ground. The word ' funeral ' had reminded her of all the myriad tasks which had to be done, and, as Dominic's secretary, she would be expected to do a good many of them. She would have to make a start for Melissa might not put in an appearance until tomorrow evening. It would look odd to do nothing for a whole day. "Who has to be notified?"

" I've written out the cables. They are on the typewriter."

Mel went over to the table where the machine was standing. She picked up the flimsy forms.

"What do I do with them?"

" I expect they can be sent over the telephone. If not someone can take them down to the cable office. It will do in the morning."

Mel glanced briefly at the cables. There were only three. Two were for the United States, one to a legal firm, the other to the President of Farrell's Frisky Fella Dog Foods. The third was for an address in Southern Ireland. It seemed very few people to notify of the death of a rich Society woman.

" Is this all?" she asked, involuntarily.

Dominic rubbed his hand over his eyes.

" Felicity's friends were hardly mine," he replied wearily. " And I don't know how many of them were real friends, at that. Her Trustees will put the usual notices in the newspapers."

" Isn't there any family?"

" Only those Irish people. I suppose a cable isn't necessary, a letter would do, but Felicity was rotten to them when her father died, and it seems only decent to let them know about—this."

" What did she do?" Mel inquired, in spite of herself, for

it was no business of hers.

"It was what she didn't do! They only heard that the old boy was dead by reading about it in a newspaper. Mrs. O'Donnell wrote her a very nice letter of condolence, with never a word of reproach. Felicity wouldn't even answer it."

"Why not?"

"She said they were just hangers-on. That letter arrived the day we set out to come here," he went on wryly. "She spent half the flight telling me that all they wanted was to find out if the old man had left them anything. That might have been so, and you couldn't really blame them because Old Man Farrell had told them as much, but they could have relied on the lawyers to be in touch with them. No, I read that letter, and it seemed to me that it was quite genuine. But Felicity wouldn't have it, so I answered it myself, without her knowledge, explaining that she was still too upset to reply in person."

"That was kind. And had Mr. Farrell left them anything?"

"He never had the chance. He didn't know of their existence until he went to Europe last Spring. His grandfather had come from Cork, originally, so he visited there to see if he could dig up any relations. Mrs. O'Donnell is the descendent of the grandfather's younger brother. I doubt if they are poor people. Her husband is a solicitor. and they have a son and daughter in university. However, I don't suppose they would have refused a legacy from their rich American cousin, and he had written to Felicity that he intended to do something for them, but he had a heart attack as he was leaving the airplane at Kennedy, and that was that."

"Bad luck for him—and them."

" They might cash in now."

" How's that?"

" Felicity was an only child, and her father tied up the money in a Trust. She received the income but could not touch the capital. I don't know much about this Trust, but I do know that if Felicity died without children—which she did—the trustees are supposed to look for distant cousins. Of course, there may be hordes of them, besides the O'Donnells."

" Don't you get anything?"

A faint smile touched Dominic's lips.

" That is the jackpot question, at least as far as the police are concerned. I don't think they believed me when I told them that, to the best of my knowledge and belief, I would not inherit a red cent."

He sounded entirely unconcerned, and Mel found such detachment slightly inhuman. Even the rich should experience a passing twinge at the loss of a handsome income. However, it was no business of hers, and resolutely she suppressed vulgar curiosity at the disposal of someone else's wealth.

" Had Mrs. Dewar no family on her mother's side?"

" None that I ever heard of. After young Aubrey's revelations tonight, I guess they came from the wrong side of the tracks and were very firmly dropped when the Farrells started going up in the world. Mrs. Farrell died just after we were married, and I don't recall any kinsfolk turning up at the funeral. Go to bed, Mel," he added. " You look done in. There is nothing more we can do tonight."

She left him huddled in a chair, sipping thoughtfully at his drink. It was the end of a very long day.

Sleep came quickly, although she had expected to lie

awake. But not for long. She woke, as suddenly as if someone had shaken her.

For a second, she thought there was another presence in
the room, a voice calling her name. But she was alone . . .

It was very dark, the only sound the soft hum of the air
conditioner. She sat up, flinging back the sheet, sweat pouring from her one moment, followed by icy shivers the next.
She was filled with a terrible dread.

She groped for the light switch, but found no comfort
in the brightness. Now the room was stifling, her breath
came with difficulty, yet, her flesh was cold to the touch
of her hands. Terror gripped her. She had never been more
afraid in her life.

To steady herself, she reached for her watch. Three-
twenty. She had slept for less than two hours. What had
happened in that short time to give her the horrors? Was it
a nightmare, forgotten on waking?

A bad dream would end with the return of consciousness,
while now waves of fear and despair engulfed her.

Suddenly, she knew what it was: Melissa! Some frightful
catastrophy threatened her twin. Melissa was in mortal
danger, and over whatever distance separated them was
sending a message.

Mel clenched her hands, knowing she was powerless to
help. The words of a childish prayer formed in her mind
and she heard her voice stammering them out.

Then it was all over, and she was shivering in the cool
artificial temperature of the room. And she knew, beyond
a shadow of a doubt, that Melissa was dead. Nothing else
could account for the intense black sense of deprivation.
That part of her being which she shared with her twin
had been torn in two.

She jumped out of bed, snatching up her dressing-gown, and ran out onto the verandah. The house as well as the guest cottage lay in darkness. She padded along to the lounge, switching on the light. The door to Dominic's bedroom was wide open, and she could not resist the urge to wake him with her terrible news. Bitterly, she thought that if he wanted proof of the sympathy which lies between identical twins, he would have it now.

His room was empty, the bed left as the maid had turned it down, his pyjamas laid neatly across his pillow.

It was then that she heard the noise: a quiet shuffling of feet, and a strange whistling, whining sound which as she listened seemed to turn into a low chanting.

In a sudden onset of nameless fear, she turned and ran.

FIVE

It was a long time till morning. Mel lay on her bed, in the dark, wondering what, if anything, she could do, and came to no satisfactory conclusion. At times, she drifted into a light sleep, when, momentarily, exhaustion overcame desolation and grief. At one point, she woke to hear a car, and then there were footsteps on the verandah, as Dominic Dewar came home, but still on her was the fear of the unseen presence whose sounds she had heard, and nothing could have induced her to leave her room. Her employer could learn of Melissa's end in the morning. Later, she slept again, and when she opened her eyes bright sunlight was edging the shutters. Her watch told her that it was eight o'clock, but she could hear none of the usual sounds of the household.

She stumbled out of bed, opened her door and looked out. There was no one to ruffle the waters of the swimming pool with their morning dip, no one walking in the shade of the flame trees, no one seated at breakfast on the terrace of the house. The cool blue water tempted her, and she slipped on her bathing suit. The swim refreshed her, setting her mind to work on her problems.

This morning, nothing seemed real. She reminded herself that it was the twenty-third of December, and that in itself felt out of joint when the sun was so hot and the garden was full of brilliant flowers and there were humming birds in the bushes. Yet her heart was like a stone within her, and that was the reality: it had not been just a bad dream, for with the coming of day, she remained convinced that Melissa was dead.

By the time she was dressed, one of the maids was busy laying the table on the verandah where she and the Dewars ate their breakfast.

"Ruby!" she said, seizing an opportunity. "Who put that grave dirt in the beds?"

For a moment the maid stared in pure terror.

"I don't know nothing about that," she gasped, and fled.

Mel sat down and waited. Ruby would have to return, with the breakfast tray. But she did not. The butler himself brought it. He gave Mel a stern look, wished her good-morning, and set the tray down in silence.

"George!"

He turned back reluctantly.

"Yes, Miss?"

"I didn't mean to frighten Ruby."

"No, Miss."

She thought she detected a softening in his face, but with that funny eye it was difficult to tell.

"Please, George, this is something we all need to know."

"Them things is best left alone, Miss, but don't you worry about it. The spirits won't harm you. Mr. French will join you for breakfast," he added, then hesitated and she thought he was on the point of saying something important. She had a sudden vivid impression that the wierd eye could see right through her pretence of being Melissa. She dismissed the idea as a product of strained nerves. There was no way that George could know.

At that moment, Justin appeared on the terrace.

"What's the matter?" he greeted her. "What has happened?"

Mel was taken aback. This man saw far too much.

"Nothing," she answered evasively, suppressing the urge to blurt it all out. "I didn't sleep much. I have some cables to send," she rushed on, to divert his attention from herself. "Can I phone them from here?"

"Give them to me. I'll have my secretary send them off."

Mel went to fetch them, glad to be away from his scrutiny if only for a moment. But he followed her into the sitting-room. She handed him the cable forms. He glanced at them, then tucked them into the pocket of his shirt.

"I see someone has been busy," he remarked.

Bewildered, Mel followed his gaze. Felicity's bedroom had been sealed by the police, a small piece of string with blobs of sealing wax to secure it stretched between door and jamb. Now a mess of mud and grass was gumming up every crevice round the frame.

"What is that?" she asked, breathless.

"To keep Felicity's duppy from getting out. The windows will have been sealed up, too."

They were. The same crude cement was stuffed into every crack.

"I heard someone, during the night. Doing that, I suppose. What is a duppy? A ghost?"

"Not as that word is understood in England. A duppy is an aparition, the form a vengeful spirit takes to make itself felt on earth. When there has been a violent death, the house of the deceased is sealed up to prevent the duppy from walking abroad."

Mel shot him a quick suspicious glance to see if he was deliberately trying to frighten her. His face told her nothing.

"Who will have done all that?"

"One of the servants," Justin said casually. "I shall not inquire."

"What are you going to do about it?"

"Nothing. If someone is so frightened that they want the room sealed, far be it from me to insist on opening it again. It can stay like that until after the funeral. The duppy will have lost its opportunity then."

"Was it the grave dirt that upset the servants?"

A faint smile touched his lips.

"Not only the servants," he reminded her.

"Mrs. French is terrified."

"My step-mother is not particularly intelligent," he replied dispassionately. "She is also White Trash, if you know what the term means. Poor whites find themselves in direct competition with the blacks for jobs, houses, you name it. They are riddled with prejudice. It's a sort of defence. They have to believe themselves superior. Don't be shocked, Mel. I quite like Vera, but I want you to know what she is. If anyone has upset the servants, it will be Vera, or Gina, who is the same as her aunt."

It flashed through Mel's mind that Lisa was right about Gina. She was wasting her time: Justin would not look twice at her. Obscurely, there was some satisfaction in the knowledge.

"Vera was good for my father," Justin went on. "And therefore, she was good for me and Dominic. She gave us a little stability. My mother died when I was fifteen, and my father was not the sort of man to live a celibate life. Until Vera showed up, we never knew whom we would

70

see at the other side of the breakfast table. She was a dancer in a night club, and my father fancied her enough to marry her. It was a highly satisfactory arrangement for all parties. Mel, you're not eating anything."

"I'm not hungry."

"Why not? Don't pretend you are grieving for Felicity. I can't imagine anyone losing a moment's sleep over her. Now you are shocked again!"

"Murder is shocking."

"Granted, though I can't imagine why someone has not had a stab at Felicity before now. That woman made more enemies than you've had hot dinners." He stopped and Mel had a swift impression that he had been about to say much more but had thought better of it. "Where's Dominic?" he asked abruptly.

"I haven't seen him this morning."

Justin left the table and disappeared inside the guest cottage.

"He's fast asleep," he announced, when he returned. "We had best leave him to rest, poor devil."

"He must be feeling her loss," Mel remarked. "Even if they were not very happy, it's a whole chunk of his life cut away."

"That wasn't what I meant," Justin retorted. "You may have noticed that I am not sentimental. Superintendent Marshall will be after him again, you may be sure. You, too, of course. The obvious suspects."

"How many times do I have to tell you—?" Mel began, but Justin interrupted her.

"You astonish me, Mel! I never thought that you had it in you. Dominic couldn't find a better defender than you. Sincerity rings in every word. How could anyone not

71

believe you?"

"You don't appear to," she retorted crossly. "I can understand that the police are going to look twice at Mr. Dewar because he was the victim's husband, but what I fail to comprehend is why you, his cousin, should accuse him."

"I don't enjoy it," Justin shot back at her.

"It doesn't make sense. He has a perfectly good alibi, and please don't go on about hired assassins. Mrs. Dewar decided to go to the beach house on the spur of the moment. He would have had to have a killer standing by, waiting for an opportune moment, and that I find far-fetched in the extreme."

A terrible thought flashed into her mind at the very moment that her tongue was denying the possibility. Dominic did have someone at hand: *Melissa.* Worse, Melissa died in the early hours of that morning, and the fear of her last moment had reached her twin. Dominic Dewar was not in his bed at the time . . .

"Apart from that," Mel raced on, to drive the idea away, "there has to be an adequate motive for murder."

"Anyone married to Felicity wouldn't be short! Don't you know what she had done to him? Tell me, what is this new book like? And how much is there of it?"

Mel was stumped. Only a few chapters existed, which was not much to show for four months' work. And they were, in Dominic's own phrase, junk.

"You see!" Justin said triumphantly. "You can't answer that, not without blowing the gaff. The book is no good, is it?"

"Not in its present form," she admitted.

"As I thought! Let me tell you a bit about Felicity. She was one of those women who marry their husbands for what

72

they are, change them, and then are dissatisfied with the result. Her first husband was a racing driver. She persuaded him to give up the game because it was too dangerous, turned him into a pen-pushing clerk in her father's business, and then wondered what had happened to the wild excitement of her romance. He never regained his position after the divorce. The last I heard of him, he was working as a mechanic. Her second was a golfer, very good, too, but these people have to be ready to travel the circuit. Felicity got bored, so no more tournaments, and very soon, no more career. The third was an opera singer, but Felicity didn't really like music and she mortally insulted the musical directors of most of the world's opera houses. That was the end of him. And then she got hold of Dominic."

"You did your homework on her," Mel commented, inadequately.

"You bet!" said Justin savagely. "So you see, if Dominic arranged for someone to stick that spear into her, good luck to him! The important point is to keep him out of the clutches of the police. Not only him, but you, too, because if Dominic set this thing up, it had to be with your connivance.

"Why?" Mel demanded, wondering what he, the police and the whole island of Jamaica would say if the truth about herself and Melissa ever came out. "You contradict your own argument, Mr. French. We all know that the last two books have been flops, and that the new book is headed in the same direction. Believe me, Dominic knows it too. He had no need to kill his wife. She was going to ditch him. All he had to do was wait a few months and then he would have been free."

"Free and poor. Dominic has no money of his own.

73

Whatever he made out of that prize-winning novel has gone, long since. Now he is back to Square One, only he is not so young as he was, and he has grown used to having a soft life. It's hard to return to conditions of years ago, and he is too proud to live on my charity, although he knows he would be welcome to it."

"But he doesn't benefit financially from Mrs. Dewar's death," Mel pointed out. "All her money was tied up in some Trust. He doesn't get anything."

Justin stared at her.

"Did Dominic tell you that? Good God, Mel, you and he must be naïve."

"Isn't it true?"

"About the Trust, yes, I imagine it is. But Felicity's personal property won't come under the terms of the Trust, and her jewellery alone must be worth a fortune. She must have made a Will, but since she hadn't any children, or close relatives, she may well have left it all to Dominic. We shall soon know. That Trustee of hers will be on the next available plane when he receives that cable. He is no friend to Dominic, and if my cousin does inherit, that old vulture will be laying down poison with the police."

George came to announce that there was a telephone call for Justin, who decided to take it in his study, and went off, leaving Mel a prey to confused and unpalatable thoughts.

She could not help but wonder if she had been taken in by Dominic Dewar, with all that that implied. She pulled herself up short. It meant that Melissa had been party to a conspiracy to *murder*. Did she really believe that was possible?

Of course, she didn't. Melissa was wild, but not *bad*. Therefore, if Dominic had contrived to kill his wife, he

74

had not done it with Melissa's help, and so he would have no need to murder her, too. Yet she was sure that her sister was dead. But she was somewhere out at sea, and accidents did happen. Perhaps her Jim wasn't as good a sailor as he imagined.

Dominic came out of the cottage, blinking at the bright sunshine. He was wearing his dressing-gown, and his hair was rumpled. He looked rather the worse for wear. He groped for the coffee pot.

"Hi, Mel!" he yawned. "What time is it?"

"Just on nine."

"Another damned day with police boots trampling all over us! Not much longer for you, though. Lucky girl! You'll be away and free by tonight."

"No," said Mel, and Dominic turned a bleary eye on her.

"No?"

"I think Melissa died in the night."

His hand jerked, spilling coffee onto the table.

"This twin thing? It really works?"

She nodded.

"Melissa knew when I broke my leg, years ago, and she was two hundred miles away at the time. I woke up in the early hours of this morning, with it coming through to me. She died hard."

"My God! But can you be sure? Couldn't it have been a bad dream? Enough happened yesterday to give anyone nightmares."

"I wish I could believe that, but I still have it this morning that she has gone."

He dabbed at the spilt coffee with a napkin.

"I sure as hell hope you are wrong," he muttered. "Melissa is a good kid. You could be mistaken, you know.

I can't believe that she won't show up at the hotel tonight."

"What do we do if she doesn't?"

"We will be stuck. We will have to sit tight and pray that that the police come up with some evidence as to the identity of Felicity's killer before poor Melissa is washed ashore. Otherwise, you and I are dead ducks. Without Melissa alive to testify where she was and prove a nice fat alibi, no one is going to believe that we didn't fix up the murder between us."

In that moment, Mel decided that her suspicions had been misplaced. If Dominic had used Melissa as his tool to dispose of his wife, he would have to be out of his head to kill her too. Melissa alive would lie for him. Melissa dead would tell a dangerous story. There had been a disaster at sea, that was all, and a dire coincidence, which could put them on the spot.

"There must be something we can do," she murmured.

"Such as what?"

"Find out where Melissa and Jim went. There must be lots of boats round these shores. If we could discover someone who has seen them, we might be able to work out where they were the day Felicity was killed."

"We could try, I guess. The snag is, Mel, that I don't know much about Melissa's Jim Brown. Wait a minute, though. I think I can identify his boat. Not its name, but the type. Hang on!"

He went back into the cottage and Mel could hear him searching through papers.

"I've got it," he announced, reappearing, a paper in his hand. "I made a note of it in case I ever wanted info. on yachting. It's an ocean-going boat, called a Tradewind. But that's all I do know. I've never actually met Jim, or laid eyes on his boat. I don't know if he lives here or is a visitor."

"He must be someone fairly local. Melissa can't have gone far outside Kingston, on her own. She didn't have a car."

"She had the use of mine every weekend, and in the evening, if she wished. Felicity encouraged her to take it," Dominic replied. "Vera put it into her head that it was infra dig or whatever to have the hired help living as family. It bugged Felicity that she hadn't thought of that for herself. They would have had Melissa eat apart, but Justin put his foot on that. So the two of them tried to freeze her out. Melissa went off as much as she could. She moved about a lot. The mileage on the clock was well up after every weekend. But I don't know where she went."

It sounded hopeless. Only the police would have the resources to track Melissa—and they would consider it a waste of time . . .

George came out of the house, bearing a silver salver with the morning post. Two letters for Dominic, and one addressed to Melissa.

"You had better open it," Dominic advised, when the butler had gone.

Mel turned the envelope over in her hands. It was cheap paper, but the handwriting was that of an educated person. Most interesting of all, it bore a local stamp, and the postmark was Port Antonio.

'Dear Mel—' she read. 'Your work is ready, and I know you want it for Christmas. Mrs. Nelson knows where it is, if you come for it when I am out. You can leave the money with her. Happy Christmas if I don't see you. Yours, Peter.'

There was no address. Just the date: December 20th.

She passed it across to Dominic.

" Peter Power," he said. " A wierdo with a beard and long hair, who is also a genius with a camera. He sells his stuff, freelance, to magazines, and he could make a name for himself if he tried. But he's happy as long as he can eat," Dominic's voice held an unconscious note of envy, " and work as he pleases. He lives at a beach chalet place, rent free in return for doing odd jobs. Melissa picked him up somewhere." He tapped the letter. " This work he mentions is for me. He took some marvellous shots of marine life, underwater, round the reefs. He has printed some up and framed them. It's Justin's Christmas present."

" Then we should fetch them."

" Today or tomorrow," Dominic agreed. " If the fuzz will let us go." His expression changed suddenly. " Mel, I've just thought: it was through Peter that Melissa met Jim."

" He might know where they were going," she exclaimed, in a sudden upbrush of hope.

" He might indeed. He could even know the name of the yacht, which would make it easier to trace," Dominic agreed, in rising excitement. " That would give us something to go on, if the worst comes to the worst."

" Let's go—now," Mel suggested.

Dominic was already on his feet.

" Why not? I can be dressed in ten minutes."

They had not reached the gates of Eagles' Nest when they found their way blocked by a police car. The driver bore a message from Superintendent Marshall, a politely worded demand for Dominic's immediate presence in his office.

" Do you think you could find your way alone?" he asked, in a low voice, as he climbed out of the car.

Mel nodded.

" Is there a map?"

" In the glove pocket. The place is The Golden Sands Chalet Park. You will see it just as you enter Port Antonio. You'll need money," he added, reaching into his hip pocket and pulling out a roll of notes.

"Wait a tick," Mel called, as he made to leave her. "This Peter. Is he Jamaican?"

"No. English, I think. Maybe Irish. White, anyway. Lots of hair. Tall and thin. Usually dressed in rags. Clean, though," he added, in fairness. " Good luck! See you later."

I hope! Mel added mentally, as she watched him driven away by the police. She followed them, slowly, to accustom herself to the unfamiliar car. She knew that she must do what she could that day. It might be their only chance. The time when either of them was free to move about the island was running out.

She found The Golden Sands Chalet Park without difficulty. It was the sort of place which sounds fine on a brochure and turns out to be a frightful disappointment. The beach was everything that was promised, and the palm trees were real enough, but the little wooden huts were run-down, and a general odour of decay pervaded the air. Once a brave venture, The Golden Sands Chalet Park was now on the skids. The tourists might have come once, Mel guessed, but not any more. It must depend on local people for its clientele, and there did not appear to be many of them at the moment. A large Vacancies notice was hung outside, creaking in the breeze off the sea.

Mrs. Nelson was in the office. She was a large, elderly woman with a yellowy-brown face, and exaggerated lipstick.

" Hi, there, honey!" she called gaily. " Peter ain't here."

" Do you know where he is?"

She lifted the flap in the counter, and came out.

" Let's have a squash," she invited, and led the way through a door at the end of the office.

Mel found herself in a hot little living-room, darkened by louvred shutters, closed against the brightness of the midday sun. Mrs. Nelson pressed a switch and a fan in the ceiling began to turn fitfully.

" Sit you down, honey," she said, waddling into the adjoining kitchen. " I'm not going to stand on no ceremony with you."

She returned with glasses of ice-cold orange.

" That's wonderful," Mel exclaimed thankfully. " You are very kind."

" Any friend of Peter's is a friend of mine," Mrs. Nelson announced, settling herself in an armchair and starting to rock herself slowly. " Like a son to me, that boy is. I miss my children, honey, but they are all in U.K., making good, every one of them. Of course, they were born there. It's home to them."

" How long were you in England," Mel asked, incautiously, and immediately wondered if Melissa would know the answer to that one.

" Twenty-five years," came the reply. " You didn't know that, did you, but then, when have you and I had a talk? You and Peter is always dashing off somewhere. Yes, twenty-five years in dear old Birmingham. I was a clippie on the buses for fifteen. Saving up, so that my Joey could come back here to retire. I don't like it all that much myself—I miss Brum and the shops, honey—and now that Joey's gone, the Good Lord look after him! I'd as soon

go back. I was real lonely until young Peter showed up."
She took a pull at her glass. " Ah, well, you don't want to
hear about an old woman like me. Not that I'd tell everyone
what I just said to you. The people round here think I'm rich
because I've lived in England and barmy because I've come
back."

" Most people dream of retiring to a place in the sun."
Mrs. Nelson laughed.

" And are bored to tears when they get there. Just like
me. You and I get along just fine, honey. But then you're
the sort of white woman who don't run a mile when she
sees a black face. Not like that pert little bitch who was here
the other day. That one wouldn't have given me so much as
the time of day if she hadn't wanted something. It was
a pleasure to tell her Peter wasn't here. ' Tell him Miss
Rawlings called,' says she, all posh. I suppose I will, 'cause
it might be business," Mrs. Nelson added regretfully.

Mel could hardly believe her ears. *Gina?*

" Was she small and blonde?"

" That's right. You know her?"

So it was Gina. But what was she doing here?

" I do."

" Friend of yours?"

" Hardly!" Mel laughed. " Has she been here before?"

" Once or twice. It must be business. Her sort would
think Peter was a bum."

" Very likely," Mel agreed, reluctantly abandoning a
dizzy thought that there might be some guilty connection between Gina and the photographer. It could only have been
business. If Melissa had recommended Peter's work to
Dominic, she could have put Gina onto him.

" If you see her, tell her he ain't back yet."

" Where is he?"

" Somewhere out on the reef, taking shots of fishes. He went a couple of days ago. He will be back tomorrow. I'm cooking him a proper Christmas dinner, with turkey and all the trimmings, and a real Jamaican Christmas pudding. You tasted one of them, yet?"

Mel shook her head.

" You don't know what you've missed! It's all raisins and rum. Peter will be back for that, for sure."

" I had a letter from him this morning. He said there were some pictures for me, and you would know where they were."

Mrs. Nelson's mouth opened in astonishment.

" That letter was for you? You Miss Grainger? Peter never calls you anything but ' Mel ' and that's a funny sort of name for a girl. That's a posh address you've got."

" Mel is short for Melissa," she trotted out the now habitual lie. " And Eagles' Nest is nothing to do with me. I'm staying there, with my boss. The photographs are for him. He is giving them as a Christmas present."

Mrs. Nelson raised her large bulk from her chair.

" We'll go get them now. You could have taken them when you was here the day before yesterday," she went on, as she led the way towards one of the other chalets, " only I didn't know you was Miss Grainger. And to tell you the truth, I forgot all about that letter. Peter gave it to me to put in the post, the morning he went, and it slipped my mind until I found it in my pocket yesterday."

Mel was scarcely listening, in the shock of realising that she had turned up a vital piece of information : Melissa had been here—on the twenty-first. The day Felicity was killed, only a few miles along the coast. That might be a step forward, but it was hardly in the right direction. It would do nothing to establish an alibi for Melissa. On the contrary, if the police discovered that Melissa had been here in Port Antonio on the day of the murder . . .

Suppressing a shudder, she waited while the door of the chalet was unlocked.

"I know just where to put my hand on them," said Mrs. Nelson. "Oh, my goodness! Look at all this!"

Mel stepped into the room. It was an unbelievable mess: furniture overturned, photographs strewn about, drawers hanging open, their contents spilling onto the floor, a cupboard door half off its hinges.

"That's the third break-in this month," Mrs. Nelson exclaimed. "Them little varmints! I'd tan their hides if I could lay my hands on them." Carefully, she stepped across the room. "You're in luck, honey. Your pictures are here, and they aren't damaged, except for the paper being torn off."

Mel made her way over to her, all but tripping over a camera. She made to pick it up, but Mrs. Nelson called out not to touch anything.

"I'll have the police here in no time, not that I need telling who done this. It's them tearaways in the town. No jobs and no money but what they steal. Though why they pick on Peter to rip off, I can't tell, seeing he ain't got much either. But he's a white man, and they think all white people have to be rich," she added, despondently.

"What about my pictures? Will I be able to take them?"

Mrs. Nelson winked.

"Why not? The police will have enough to go at without them. I'll pack them up for you again," she said and tucked them under her arm.

Mel turned to follow her out, picking her way amongst Peter Power's scattered possessions. Examples of his work were pinned over most of the walls. Mel was no judge, but it looked very competent stuff. One by the door caught her eye: it was a simple, yet subtle composition, a woman standing by a palm tree, her back to the camera, staring out to sea. A lovely thing, with a haunting quality about it. Moreover, it was a photograph of Felicity Dewar.

SIX

Mel called Mrs. Nelson back.

" Do you know who this is?" she asked.

Mrs. Nelson glanced at the photograph.

" Some chick," she shrugged.

" Has she ever been here?"

" I never seen her." She peered more closely. " I think Peter done this a couple of weeks ago. I seem to recall it as one of a batch he showed me. Thought he might sell it to some magazine. Pretty, ain't it?"

" It's beautiful. He didn't think of selling it to the woman who posed for it?"

" I don't suppose he knowed who she was, honey. He goes all over the island, hopping on buses, and taking photos when he feels like it. ' Finding a subject ' he calls it. He could have taken that one the other side of the island."

But he had not. Mel recognised the setting at first glance : the photograph had been taken outside Justin French's beach house. Yet she was satisfied that Mrs. Nelson had never laid eyes on Felicity Dewar in the flesh.

" I'll ask him when he comes back," she said in what she hoped was a careless tone. " I might know someone who would like a print of it," she added, thinking of Dominic, who, no matter what his cousin said, must be feeling the loss of his wife. " In any case, I want a word with Peter.

If I leave my phone number, would you ask him to call me?"

"Sure thing, honey," Mrs. Nelson promised.

Mel walked slowly out to her car, leaving the owner of the Golden Sands Chalet Park reporting the break-in to the police and fairly making the telephone wires hum with her comments on idle youths. She had much food for thought. She had come to Port Antonio in search of information and she could not complain that she had not obtained it.

Melissa had been in Port Antonio on the day of the murder, which was bad news in a way. Yet it meant that she did not have to waste precious hours in fruitless searching all over Jamaica. If Melissa had come here, it must have been to join Jim, since that was the day they had gone off in the boat. Add to that two more facts—that Peter Power lived here, and that it was through him that Melissa had met Jim—and it was reasonable to conclude that Jim lived, or spent much of his time, in this very town. Her spirits rose. It should not be all that difficult to trace him. She need not wait for Peter to return. A few questions at the harbour might provide her with a description of the boat, and, with luck, some idea of where it had been heading.

There was another car parked behind her own, in the trees bordering the edge of Mrs. Nelson's property. Mel glanced at it idly, then stopped short.

It was Justin French's Mercedes, chauffeur at the wheel, and its owner emerging from it. The first glimpse of his face caused Mel to brace herself for storms.

"What are you doing here?" he demanded.

She was glad that she had a genuine excuse for her trip.

"I've been collecting some pictures for Mr. Dewar," she replied, indicating her parcel.

"Pictures? At a time like this? Whatever next?"

"I understand they are for your Christmas present," she retorted, and had the satisfaction of seeing him taken aback.

"Oh, I see," he said inadequately, but his eyes were still bright with suspicion.

"There was a letter this morning saying the pictures were ready," she went on, feeling that Justin might have a right to some explanation, for it did look odd for Dominic to be thinking about pictures the morning after finding his wife murdered. "Mr. Dewar is with the police so I came over to pick them up. The photographer lives here."

"I know."

It seemed that everyone at Eagles' Nest was acquainted with Peter Power. She was treading upon dangerous ground, for her own knowledge of the man was sketchy, and she, of all people, might be expected to know all about him.

"How did you know I was here?" she asked, to divert his attention.

Justin let out a short, humourless laugh.

"Do me a favour! Allow me to recognise a car which has been garaged at my house for the past four months, and the hiring of which I arranged."

Mel flushed.

"I'm sorry. I didn't think."

"You mean, you didn't expect to be seen here today." The suspicion was back in his voice, and Mel could hardly blame him. She guessed she was a rotten bad actor: her ulterior motive must stick out a mile.

"Have you had lunch?" he asked abruptly.

She shook her head.

"Neither have I. Salvation!" he called, beckoning the chauffeur. He took the pictures from her and handed them to the man. "Take Mr. Dewar's car and go home. Give him this parcel and tell him Miss Grainger will ride back with me."

Helplessly, Mel watched Salvation drive away in her car. She was stuck with Justin French now—and his questions —all the way back to Kingston. She took her place in the passenger seat of the Mercedes because there was nothing else to do.

But it seemed that they were not going directly home. Justin drove back into Port Antonio, then swung off to the left, away from the little town and in the opposite direction to the beach house.

"There is a place along here where the food is quite good," he said, by way of explanation. "There is no hurry to go back home. Nothing but trouble there," he added with a twisted smile.

An idiotic thought presented itself to Mel's mind: there was a certain undefined pleasure in being driven along in a luxurious car by a man who was—at last she faced the fact— quite devastatingly attractive.

"Is there any news?" she asked, forcing herself to concentrate on the word 'trouble'. "I haven't seen anyone this morning except you and Dom—I mean, Mr. Dewar."

"Let's drop the formalities, at least when you are with me. I've noticed you are scrupulously correct in addressing all of us, Mel, but it doesn't protect you from gossip. Besides, you are one of the family."

Mel stiffened.

"I'm not planning on marrying Dominic, now that he is free!" she snapped.

Justin laughed.

"Of course not! That wasn't what I meant at all, but

it was bad taste to tease you, after what you have had to take from the police and my dear stepmother, not to mention the late unlamented Felicity."

"Justin!" Mel protested, then flushed as he laughed again.

"You said that very nicely, just as if you had been practising! Ah, but I am teasing you again, and you are right to rebuke me. It is deplorable to speak ill of the dead no matter how true it is. May her faults rest with her! Shall we cry Pax?" he added, reaching out for her hand and carrying it briefly to his lips.

"Yes," Mel gasped, hardly able to speak for the sudden thumping of her heart which seemed to have jumped right up into her throat. She stared straight out of the windscreen, not daring so much as to glance at him. At any minute, she knew, she could make a complete fool of herself. As if she were not in sufficient trouble!

The ' place where the food is quite good ' turned out to be an exclusive haven for the idle rich, built in the style of an old plantation Great House, complete with shady colonades, and giving onto its own private beach. They ate on the terrace, beneath a striped awning, while a steel band played for, apparently, their sole pleasure.

"There are very few people about," Mel remarked. "Where are they all?"

"The tourist trade is in a bad way this year," Justin told her. "One of our major industries, too. It's all the unrest, of course. And the thought of Cubans being here frightened the Americans away."

"Cubans? Here?"

"That's the name of the game in Caribbean economic co-operation, these days. However, it doesn't mean that we are going to live in Russia's pocket. We want to do things our way, but we have to accept help where it is offered. That is Lesson Number One, Mel," he added, with a half-smile. " It will do for today. Tell me, how well do you know Peter Power?"

Mel took a deep breath. She would far rather discuss the Cuban presence than the photographer, but she was not being given the choice.

" He's an acquaintance," she said casually. She hoped that was true: Melissa had not so much as mentioned him. But then she had not spoken of Jim, either, and clearly *he* was more than a face in the crowd. " He's a very good photographer," she added, hoping to draw Justin onto safer ground.

" Naturally," he replied. " Felicity was never interested in anyone second rate."

Mel gaped at him.

" Felicity?"

" Didn't you realise? I'm not a hundred per cent certain, but I think this Peter is the one she used to meet at the beach house."

" How do you make that out?"

" Look at the facts. We know Felicity had a boy friend somewhere round here. Dominic suspected it, and she virtually admitted it to me when I taxed her with it. So who could it be? Felicity never went for an ordinary bloke. He had to be somebody different, with some special talent, to give her a bit of reflected glory."

" But Peter isn't famous."

" He's on his way up. Don't be fooled by his appearance. He had a spread in the National Geographic not so long ago. Very remarkable stuff. Felicity's sort of meat, and I expect she dazzled him with promises of all the contacts she could make for him."

Mel thought about it. It fitted.

"There is a photograph of her in his room."

"Imagine that!" Justin exclaimed. "We have been looking for some connection between them."

"We?"

"Myself and Tib Morley. As soon as I began to suspect that Felicity was meeting someone, I had Tib start a few inquiries in Port Antonio. That is what he and Lisa were doing there yesterday when we found Felicity. We didn't know where to start looking for the boy friend, but we knew there could not be an unlimited number of talented young men on that stretch of the coast, and white, of course, for Felicity. The biggest black talent in the world wouldn't have overcome her Southern prejudices. Tib had turned up Peter Power, but we had not been able to establish a connection between him and Felicity."

"You have gone to a great deal of trouble."

"I was trying to help Dominic. Felicity liked to be the injured party in her divorces, so that there was no settlement for the discarded husband. I intended to play her at her own game. She was aiming to manufacture evidence against Dominic, using you or someone else, no doubt, if you proved useless. I meant to get something on her, so that she would have to make a financial arrangement before she could have her divorce. For once she was going to have to pay for the pleasure."

"Would Dominic have accepted a pay off?"

"I doubt it," Justin said with a laugh. "He's too soft. But it would have been a pleasure to see Felicity wriggling on the end of a hook. Not that any of it matters now. Unless we can come up with a reason why Peter Power might have wanted her dead."

"He wasn't in Port Antonio the day she was killed. He had gone off to some reef the day before to take photographs. He is due back tomorrow."

"That doesn't rule him out," Justin remarked. "It could be some sort of alibi. But, agreed, he's not a likely candidate. It was in his interest to keep her alive. He couldn't know what she would do to him once they were married."

Not for the first time, the harshness of his judgement of the dead woman jarred on Mel.

"Can't you give her the credit for ever falling in love?"

A grim smile touched Justin's lips.

"Oh, Felicity thought she was in love, every time. And maybe she was, in her own way. It was her idea of marriage that was all wrong. She wanted everything done her way."

"You don't believe in the wife wearing the pants?" Mel challenged him, unable to resist a poke at him, a dominant male if ever there was one.

She saw an answering glint in his eyes, but he refused to be drawn.

"Not when it means the sacrifice of the husband's career," he said seriously. "If a man is doing a job he loves, it is a part of him, and anyone who tries to drag him away from it is dismembering him. Women like Felicity never understand that. They are spiders: they eat their mates. It's time we were off," he went on, abruptly, as if he regretted opening up some little part of his mind to her. "I've a phone call to make. Wait for me at the car."

He strode off into the hotel, leaving Mel to follow him. She found her way to the Powder Room, and spent a few minutes trying ineffectually to reduce the shine on her nose. It was a lost cause, in the heat of the day, and she gave up. She was about to leave, when the door opened to admit a girl she had seen behind the Reception Desk.

"Hallo, Miss Grainger," she said pleasantly, with the ease of an acquaintance of some standing. "I thought you had gone to the Virgin Islands."

"Tomorrow," Mel told her, thinking that the Virgin Islands might as well be on the moon, for all the chance she stood of flying there in the morning.

"Have a good trip. A week, isn't it? I'll hold your room for you the next weekend. Not that we are likely to have a full house, this year," she added wryly.

So this was one of Melissa's weekend haunts! Mel blessed the chance that had brought Justin French to Port Antonio in time to catch her at the Chalet park. She might never have dropped on this place, left to herself. And if Melissa came here every weekend, the chances were that Jim would not be far away, might even be a fellow guest. The snag was that she could not pump this girl about Jim without admitting that she was not Melissa. But it was all useful information—for someone else to work on, if the need arose.

"Did you find the garage you were looking for, the other day?" the girl was saying.

"Yes, thanks," Mel replied faintly, as her mind worried at the words.

Melissa had been here recently. That had to mean on the day of the murder, when she called on Mrs. Nelson. And she was driving an unknown car, which must now be garaged somewhere nearby. This was real meat. Melissa's trail should be easy to pick up now.

She itched to get on with the job, seek out the garage,

93

and take it from there—but there was no way of getting rid of Justin, and she would have no transport if she did.

" I suppose you haven't seen Mr. Power?" the girl asked, as they went out into the corridor together. " The boss is hopping mad because he was due here this morning to take some shots for the art work on next year's brochure, but he never showed up."

" He's gone off to some reef. Mrs. Nelson is expecting him back tomorrow."

" He must have forgotten. And I thought he needed the bread! I'll call her and ask her to remind him."

A cold finger touched Mel's spine. Would the photographer have forgotten a professional engagement? What was it Dominic had said? If Felicity's boy friend had been with her when the assassin came up with her, he wouldn't be left alive, but fed to the fishes. She hoped that Peter Power really was cruising happily round a reef, photographing marine life.

Justin was in one of the phone booths in the foyer. As she passed him, he replaced the receiver and came out.

" No one wants either of us," he announced. " I called the house, my office and Tib Morley. Dominic is back home and the police are nowhere in evidence. Let us hope they have some sort of lead which takes them away from Eagles' Nest. We are meeting Tib and Lisa for dinner, but until then our time is our own. I thought we would drive around the mountains a bit."

Mel had the idea that she was being hijacked. It was a most pleasurable sensation. Possibly Justin's aim was to keep her away from Dominic, or scotch gossip, but that did not lessen the excitement of the company of an attractive man. It was a long time since she had been free to go out

94

with anyone.

Justin knew the mountains well, taking her away from the beaten track to see hidden waterfalls, opening up before her eyes views the average tourist never saw. He told her bits of folklore, and snippets of the island's history, with his own love of the place shining through at every word.

It came to her that she envied him in this. She had no great sense of belonging to the industrial town where she had lived all her life. Perhaps that was what was wrong with her. Her attachment had been to family and friends, but with her parents dead, and her closest friend proved false, there was nothing left to hold her. With Melissa gone, too, there was nowhere she could call 'home.'

" I don't think I have any roots," she said aloud, her guard down for a moment.

" It's possible to grow them, when you find a place to put them down," he replied. " My ancestor was a footloose, nameless French adventurer, a pirate for all I know, who fetched up here sometime in the late sixteenth century. He ingratiated himself with the Spaniards, married a lady with some property, and put down roots. We have been here ever since. We have lived under the Spaniards, and then the English. We have made our living, trading and carrying goods between the islands, and now we dabble in industry. There have been good times and bad. I don't know what the future holds, but this is my home and here I stay. I am no expatriate to be driven out by nationalists," he added fiercely, and broke the spell which had made the afternoon a time apart.

A cloud drifted across the face of the sun.

" Dominic thinks Felicity was killed by extremists," she said, " as a means of attacking you."

"It is possible," Justin agreed.

"Have there been threats?"

He laughed.

"To me and most other prominent businessmen on the island. We don't take any notice, apart from making sure that no one can break into our houses. I have men with guard dogs patrolling at night at Eagles' nest. They are on duty in daytime, now. I can't risk anyone else being killed, if, indeed, that was why Felicity died."

Mel interpreted his tone rather than his words.

"You don't think so?"

"No. These people wouldn't need to take one of my harpoons. They have their own weapons. An M16 rifle is more the ticket. I'm sorry, Mel, but there isn't an easy way out of this one. It would be great to pin it on an outsider, but so far we don't know of anyone, apart from the boy friend, who had contact with Felicity." He glanced at his watch. "It's time we headed for home, if we are not to keep the Morleys waiting tonight. It's a good hour's drive, and we must change."

Mel had ceased trying to figure out why Justin wanted to keep her with him. The most likely explanation was that it was all part of some plan to keep Dominic out of gaol, but she caught herself pretending that it was for the pleasure of her company. Undeniably, she liked being with him— she could have wished that the afternoon would never end— and the prospect of dining out was delightful . . .

It took well over the hour to reach Eagles' Nest, for the road was partially blocked from a landslip in a storm a few days back.

"Forty minutes!" said Justin. "Can you be ready?"

It sounded almost like a test.

"Yes," she replied, and fled to the guest cottage.

She stood in the shower, hastily washing off the accumulated sweat of the day, and wondering which of Melissa's dresses would become her most. Her twin's taste was for brighter colours than her own, but she had noticed a yellow dress in the wardrobe, which she might have chosen for herself. She was so intent on making the best of herself that she did not hear a light knock on her door, nor did she hear it open.

"I knew you must be here, because the light was on," said a voice accusingly. "I did knock."

Mel swung round from the mirror.

Gina was standing in the doorway, looking anything but pleased. She took in the yellow dress and the careful make-up, and her eyes narrowed.

"May I come in?"

"Oh, please do," Mel muttered, recovering herself. "I'm sorry. I didn't hear you."

Gina sat down in the armchair, carefully arranging herself to the best advantage, as was her habit. Mel was fascinated: she had noted the little ritual before, and assumed it was party manners, or bait-laying for any men who happened to be around. To go through it in another girl's bedroom argued that it was automatic.

"A new dress?" Gina inquired.

To her annoyance, Mel felt herself flush. Her visitor's tone did not lead her to expect a compliment.

"Not particularly. I'm going out."

"So I understand. You have been out all day. With Justin."

"I met him, by accident, that's all. He was kind enough to take me for a drive in the mountains."

"And he is taking you out to dinner tonight?"

"With the Morleys," Mel returned, feeling her temper rising. It did not require a genius to work out why this girl favoured her with a visit.

"Those blacks!" Gina exclaimed contemptuously.

"I like them," Mel said shortly. She looked at her watch. "I'm sorry, I have to go."

She made for the door, leaving Gina to follow or stay as she wished.

"Mel!"

Reluctantly, she turned back.

"Yes?"

Gina was on her feet.

"One little word before you leave." Her voice was cold. "It seems that I under-estimated you, but let's get one thing clear right now. I'm not giving up Justin to you. You may do what you like with Dominic. It's nothing to me that you and he contrived to get rid of Felicity. I don't know how you did it, but there must be some way of breaking that alibi of yours, because I saw you driving a green car on the road to Port Antonio that day, when you were supposed to be at that conference. I haven't told the police yet, but I will, if you don't make it clear to Justin that you don't like his company. Go and enjoy your dinner, Mel, and remember what I have said. Make sure you do it tonight."

SEVEN

Mel stood watching Gina walk over to the house, although she knew that the seconds were ticking away and Justin would be waiting for her. Then she was aware of another presence, and glanced round.

"I heard that," said Dominic, from the door of the sitting-room. "Could she have seen Melissa?"

"Oh, yes. I found out a good deal more than I bargained for, today. Melissa was in Port Antonio, and at a place called the Planters' Inn. I have the impression that she stayed there most weekends, though it looks very expensive."

"Those hotels give special terms for residents," Dominic told her, "and Felicity gave her a raise to cover extra expenses while we were here."

"Felicity?"

His mouth twisted wryly.

"She paid the bills. You don't imagine that I could afford to pay a secretary, do you?"

"Did she pay for my trip, too?"

"Indirectly. I told her it was for some special research. Which it was, too!"

"Do you really mean to write this book?"

"Why not? Good God, Mel," he said, wounded, "I didn't drag you all the way here just to rig up my wife's murder!"

99

Mel shook her head.

" I'm sorry! This is a corrosive business. I am beginning to suspect everyone."

" Then try suspecting Gina," Dominic recommended. " If she saw Melissa on the Port Antonio road, then she has lied to the police about her own movements. If I remember rightly, she said she was shopping in Kingston. Unfortunately, we can't expose her without landing ourselves in trouble."

" It doesn't seem to bother her that we might do just that. I think she was in Port Antonio herself that day. Mrs. Nelson said she came looking for Peter after he had gone. But, then, Gina hasn't any visible motive for wanting to kill Felicity. She makes it amply clear that your wife was more or less a stranger to her."

" I wonder!" Dominic replied unexpectedly. " For a stranger, Felicity was mighty upset at the idea of Gina marrying Justin. If you ask me, I reckon she would have done anything to put a stop to it."

A thought popped into Mel's mind: had Gina some grounds for complaint against her? Was she dreaming, albeit ever so vaguely, of supplanting her, as Helen, her once-best friend, had taken her own place in Scott's affections? Common sense brought her up short: the chance would be something! Nevertheless, she voiced the question uppermost in her mind.

" And is Justin going to marry Gina?"

Dominic shrugged.

" I shouldn't think so! As I told Felicity, but she wouldn't have it. She couldn't bring herself to give me any credit for powers of observation. She held that a determined woman can always get her man. She should have known of course!"

At that moment, Justin himself appeared on the terrace at the other side of the pool.

"I must go," Mel said hurriedly, and walked quickly over to him, forgetting Dominic and Gina and everyone else in a sudden rush of pleasure at seeing him.

Careful! she warned herself. Idle dreams were not to be taken for reality. Her whole relationship to Justin was based on a falsehood. She would do well to remember that.

His words of greeting dispelled what remained of her pleasure.

"You were talking to Dominic. What about?"

Suspicion was as common as daily bread in this house, Mel thought, feeling the bump of coming back to earth.

"We don't conspire every time we meet," she said acidly.

But they did. That was the awful part of it. Lies breeding yet more lies.

It occurred to her that it would not be difficult to obey Gina's command. She was unlikely to enjoy Justin's company that evening, and there was no reason to conceal the fact.

The Morleys were waiting for them at a quiet restaurant in the foothills of the mountains, on the road above Constant Spring. There were few other diners, and they had a secluded corner to themselves. Since it was also very dark, with only red-shaded lamps to cast a doubtful light at the tables, they could have almost complete privacy.

Mel soon discovered that it was not intended to be a purely social evening, and decided that Justin had chosen to meet his friends here to be away from listening ears in his own home.

"Well?" Justin demanded, as soon as they were settled at their table and had ordered. "Did you find anything?"

Tib Morley nodded.

"I am stuffed with information like an egg with meat. Superintendent Marshall smiles on me, although he knows I am retained by you. The man feels he needs help, but can hardly say so. He wants this thing wrapped up quickly, before the American ambassador starts making noises. The Tourist Board is already on his back."

"Naturally," Justin snorted. "Things are bad enough without visitors getting themselves killed. I imagine he would like to bring it home to one of us."

"Sure thing!" Tib grinned back at him. He rolled an eye towards Mel. "You and Dominic are his prime suspects, young lady. It bites him that he can't shake your alibis, but he is looking round for a hireling. You see there is one item in both your testimonies which doesn't fit with other evidence."

"What's that?" asked Mel, her mouth suddenly dry. It was now crystal clear to her why Justin had brought her along. To be grilled by Tib Morley in a place where Dominic could not come to her aid.

"You both state that you didn't know that Felicity was not going with you to the conference until the morning of the day itself."

"That's right. She sprang it on us at breakfast."

"Yet she sent word to the kitchen that she would need a picnic basket *the night before*," Tib said, studying her.

Mel looked round the table. Their faces were in semi-shadow. But not hers. She had been placed by the lamp, where they all could see her.

"I didn't know that. I don't know why she didn't tell us the night before, but she did not. Does it matter?"

"Oh, yes. If Dominic had hired someone to kill her,

there would be that much more time to make the last minute arrangements."

Mel leant forward.

"Doesn't it work both ways? Why couldn't it mean that Felicity was meeting someone at the beach house and didn't want her husband to suspect?"

"I told you she has a head on her shoulders," Justin put in. "I would prefer to think she is right."

"That's something!" Mel snapped.

Justin frowned.

"You should know by now that I am on your side!"

"Thanks very much for nothing," Mel returned, now beyond caring. "You think your cousin and I fixed this thing up and you want to help us get away with it. I, for one, can do without that sort of assistance. Why don't you try believing that we are innocent?"

There was a short, difficult silence, relieved by the arrival of the waiter with the first course.

"What else have you got, Tib?" Justin inquired, when the man had gone.

"The results of the autopsy, if you don't mind discussing it while we eat," Tib replied, with a swift glance at his wife.

Justin had no time for female sensibilities.

"Get on with it, man!"

"Very well. Death occurred somewhere between ten a.m. and six in the evening, with the likelihood of it being in the morning. The contents of the stomach show only breakfast eaten. Did you know she was pregnant?"

"What?"

"So you didn't. Maybe she didn't, either. It was in the very early stages."

" The doctor's appointment!" Mel broke in.

" That's right," Tib confirmed. " He was going to do a test. That's just about all from the autopsy, except that she died very quickly. The weapon pierced the heart." He paused, then went on, " which brings us to what I have gleaned from the police. There are no fingerprints on the spear or the gun which fired it. Both very carefully wiped clean. There are plenty of fingerprints at the beach house, including one set which has not been identified. What are your cleaning and security arrangements there, Justin?"

" The place is kept locked up when we are not using it. Shutters on the windows and a high fence round the property. There is a man from the village who keeps an eye on it, does the garden, and his wife cleans through once a week. I don't know how thorough she is. Those unidentified prints could be from some guest we had there. It depends where they were found."

" On a door in one of the changing rooms."

" That could be it. The cleaner will only wash the floor in there in the normal way."

Tib nodded, fetched a notebook out of his pocket and scribbled a line in it.

" There is no sign of any break-in at the beach house. Whoever took that spear was either let in by Felicity or had a key. Or Felicity herself might have taken the gun and spear herself. If she did, her fingerprints were wiped off along with those of her murderer."

" Where was she killed?" Justin asked.

" Where you found her. There is no sign that the body was moved. The Superintendent's theory is that she was killed as she stepped out of the boat that brought her to the creek. The murderer stood in the boat and shot her

104

down."

" My boat?"

Tib turned his hand expressively.

" That's anyone's guess. Let's put it this way: that boat hadn't been wiped clean of fingerprints, nor are there any prints on it which shouldn't be there. Apart from Felicity's own, those that are on it belong to you, Dominic, Vera, Gina, Aubrey and Mel. In other words, your present household. No trace of anyone else."

Mel experienced a surge of relief. If Justin's boat had conveyed Felicity and her murderer to the creek, then Melissa had no part in the crime. Twins did not share fingerprints and of the two of them, only hers were in that boat.

" Gloves?" Lisa suggested, joining in the conversation for the first time.

Tib shook his head.

" In this climate? So far the theory is that Felicity and her murderer travelled to the creek together. If he or she had been wearing gloves it would have seemed a bit odd. Besides, if the murderer had worn gloves there would have been no need to wipe the weapon."

" So where does all this leave us?" Justin inquired.

Tib shrugged.

" If your boat was used, then one of you did it. If it wasn't, the field is wide open again, the only limitation being: whom did Felicity know well enough to go off with on a supposedly scuba-diving expedition."

" The boy friend," said Justin.

" Obviously. Whoever he is."

" I thought you had decided he was this photographer, Peter Power?"

Tib shook his head.

" I only suggest him as a strong possibility, for the simple reason that I haven't turned up anyone else in the locality of Port Antonio who might have attracted Felicity's attention. But there are two snags. One is this young man's appearance: very hairy, bare-footed, ragged jeans and T-shirt. I can't imagine Felicity not changing that even before she married him. And the other is that I have not yet established any connection between them. For all I know, they never set eyes on each other."

" Mel says there is a photograph of Felicity in Power's room."

Tib made another note in his book.

" With ' All my love, Felicity ' written across it, I hope?"

Mel shook her head

" Nothing like that. It's one of those works of art which looks so simple until you try to do one. Just a woman on a beach with her back half-turned to the camera, as if she didn't know it was there. But I think it was taken near the beach house."

" I'll get after it," Tib promised, " though I should warn you, Justin, that I could be flogging a dead horse. It was in the boy friend's interest for Felicity to be alive, not dead. I doubt if she had got round to leaving him anything in her Will. She can't have known him very long."

" Dead horse or not, Tib, it's the only one we have."

" What I don't understand," said Lisa, suddenly, " is why the murderer bothered to return the gun to the beach house. Why not leave it by the body?"

" Have the police any theories on that?" Justin inquired.

" I'm not that much in Superintendent Marshall's confidence," Tib replied. " It seems an unnecessary risk to go back to the beach house. Unless it was the first mistake in an otherwise well-laid plan. The murderer wouldn't want to be hanging around at the creek, once Felicity was dead, and maybe he didn't realise that he—or she!—still had the gun until later. But in that case it would have been more sensible to throw the thing overboard. On the other hand, there is another alternative."

"What?" Justin demanded.

Tib eyed him.

"You aren't going to like this, but it must have occurred to the police. If the murderer was someone living in your house, there was no risk involved in being seen at the beach house, and the gun could have been put back for the purpose of concealing the crime. You might overlook a missing spear, but not a missing gun."

There was a short silence.

"It comes back, every time, to one of us, doesn't it?" Justin said, at last. He glanced at Mel. "You must be very thankful that you have an iron-clad alibi."

Mel looked across at him, startled. For one heart-stopping moment she thought that he *knew.* But he was not watching to see her betray herself. He had turned away and was signalling to the waiter.

She was glad when the uncomfortable meal was over and they were back at Eagles' Nest, where she could escape to the guest cottage. There was a light on in the sitting-room, and she could hear the sound of the typewriter. She hesitated for a while, then went in.

Dominic was working. All round him were the visible signs of an author plying his trade: bits of paper with notes scribbled on them, the waste paper basket full to overflowing, and a small pile of typescript.

She stood and stared. What a moment for inspiration to begin to flow!

" Ah, you're back," he said cheerfully. " Enjoy your dinner?"

" Not much. It was a strictly business meeting with our legal adviser. I learnt quite a lot tonight, none of it either pleasant or encouraging."

" Such as?"

She looked at him with compassion.

" I don't know that I am the right person to break this to you. I'm afraid you have lost more than your wife. You have lost a child, too."

Dominic stared.

" Felicity was pregnant?"

" It was in the very early stages. You didn't know?"

He shook his head.

" I can't believe it. Felicity never wanted children. In any case," he said bleakly, " it is not my loss. There is no way that child could be mine. However, it confirms the existence of the boy friend and that it was a heavy romance. Melissa hasn't shown up yet," he added, changing the subject abruptly. " I called the hotel half an hour ago."

Mel's heart missed a beat, and she realised how much she had hoped that her instinct was wrong, that the telepathic experience of the early hours had been nothing but a bad dream.

" What are we going to do?" A new thought struck her. " All my luggage is at that hotel, not to mention the papers for the settlement of Dad's estate which I brought with me for Melissa to sign, and my passport, too."

" I've been thinking about that. There is only one thing for it. You will have to go down there tomorrow morning,

108

pay the bill, clear the room, and ask them to keep the luggage for a while. Tell them you are going off on a trip, and don't want to cart it all with you."

" I have to find out what has happened to Melissa."

" Maybe she will turn up, right as rain, tomorrow morning," he said in a tone of deep gloom which belied the optimism of his words. " I've had an idea how we can trace her Jim. According to Melissa that yacht of his is just about the last word in its class—and a pretty new design. There can't be all that many of them around. I've cabled a friend in New York, asking him to find out where the Tradewind is built, and to get hold of a list of the people who have bought one. Then we can find her registration and her name. She shouldn't be all that difficult to trace in these waters, even as a wreck."

For what good it may do us! Mel thought. The fact that Melissa had driven to Port Antonio on the day of the murder was sufficient to damn the lot of them. Without Melissa alive to give her testimony, the circumstantial evidence could swamp them. Why couldn't Melissa have stuck to the arrangements? They need never have been in this mess.

She crushed down the spurt of irritation. Her twin was dead, and her faults had died with her. Depressed, she went to bed.

Straight after breakfast, Dominic drove her to the hotel in Constant Spring. It was gay with decorations and Mel remembered that it was Christmas Eve. Heavy-hearted, she packed up the luggage, while Dominic paid the bill. Her cases were stowed in the hotel storeroom, ready for her to collect when—*if*, she thought with a shiver—she was free to leave the island. Even then, she was going to be in difficulties.

"Melissa took my passport with her," she announced, as they drove away.

Dominic frowned.

"Did she?" Then his face cleared. "Hey! That means they intended to leave Jamaican waters. I hope to God they did! If they were wrecked off some other island, there is no reason why the police should ever find out that there were two of you—and our precious Gina can tell all Kingston that she saw you on that road, and no one will believe her."

Mel thought it over. He was right! Relief swept over her, and with it a sense of shame. It seemed callous to hope that poor Melissa and her Jim had perished outside the jurisdiction of the Jamaican police. Yet facts were facts— and she would be very thankful indeed to be spared embarrassing explanations, not only to the police, but to Justin French.

"I promise you," said Dominic, "that when all this has blown over, we will search the Caribbean, if necessary, to find Melissa's body, and give her a decent burial. If that is any comfort."

It was, in an oblique fashion.

Justin pounced on them the moment they reached Eagles' Nest.

"Where have you been?" he demanded, but did not wait for an answer. "The office has sent up the replies to your cables, Dominic. Those Irish cousins want to be represented at the funeral. It seems that the son is on holiday in Antigua. We are to let him know date and place. And there is one from Felicity's Trustee. He will be arriving on the evening of the twenty-sixth, but he wants you to call him today. He will be at his office until four o'clock, New York time, so you had better get that call booked. There may be a delay. He will have had a look at the Will, and there are sure to be funeral instructions. The inquest is set for nine a.m. on the twenty-seventh, and they will release the body for burial. The mortician is here. He is waiting for you in my study."

Dominic looked daunted, and went into the house without a word.

"Well?" said Justin. "Where did you go?"

"Only down into Kingston to do an errand," Mel told him, feeling hunted.

She hurried through the hall, with him close behind. He was still with her when she reached the guest cottage. She resigned herself to the fact that he could not be shaken off, and wondered what further inquisition was in store for her.

She was not to find out. Relief came in the shape of Vera French, high-heeled sandals clicking angrily on the flagstones of the terrace. Behind her, almost at a run to keep up, were Gina and Aubrey.

"Justin!"

"What is it, Vera?" he said warily.

She opened her mouth to speak, but at that moment caught sight of the mud and grass daubed round the windows of Felicity's room.

"My God! What's that?"

A glint of devilment appeared in Justin's eyes.

"Someone wants to keep the duppies from getting out. Shall I scrape it off?"

She turned on him.

"You are unspeakably callous! For heaven's sake, leave it alone. *You* haven't had grave dirt put in your bed! You

111

don't care what happens to any of us. I suppose it is no news to you that our laundry woman's father is an Obeahman?"

"No," he replied calmly. "I knew that. When did you find out?"

"This minute. Aubrey told me. It seems that my own son thinks so little of his mother that he never thought fit to mention it to the police. And neither did you, I suppose?"

Justin glared at his step-brother.

"Did you have to tell her that?"

"It just slipped out," Aubrey admitted miserably.

"Then it is about time you learned to keep your mouth shut. No, Vera, I did not tell the police. And I suggest that you do not, either. That grave dirt had nothing to do with Felicity's death."

"Perhaps you will change your tune when Gina and I and Mel are all dead! What are you going to do about that woman?"

"Nothing."

Vera could not believe her ears.

"You mean, you are going to keep her on?"

"Certainly. She is a good worker. She is also a respectable church-going woman, who has four children to keep and a drunken layabout of a husband. She depends on her work to feed her family. I will not have you interfering with my staff, Vera. If you are afraid of Pleasant Jackson, then I suggest that you remove to an hotel."

Mel could not resist a glance at Gina. The last thing she would want was to be obliged to leave Eagles' Nest, and she could hardly stay if her aunt left. Mel wondered how she would stop Vera.

Gina took her cue.

"Auntie Vee," she said sweetly. "I'm sure you can trust Justin. He knows this woman, and we don't."

Vera's eyes swept scornfully round the assembled company.

"I'd go this minute, if I thought it would do any good. Justin, that spell must be taken off us. Fetch that woman here and tell her!"

He sighed and crossed to the bell-push. The butler appeared with a speed which suggested to Mel that he had been listening. She searched his face for confirmation but, with that strange eye of his, could not tell.

"George," said Justin. "Please ask Pleasant to come here."

She was a real Black Mammy, with a bright scarf tied round her hair and a dress patterned with huge scarlet flowers. Her round face was troubled, and already there were tears in her eyes. She stood before Justin and trembled.

"Don't upset yourself, Pleasant," he said, more gently than Mel would have believed possible. "Mrs. French is bothered about the grave dirt, and she has heard about your father."

Pleasant wept openly.

"I don't see my Daddy for years! He a bad man. I don't know nothing about the grave dirt."

"I never thought that you did. You tell Mrs. French that and it will put her mind at rest."

Mel's attention was distracted by a flicker of movement on the terrace at the other side of the pool. One of the maids was there, and behind her Superintendent Marshall, accompanied by a plain clothes man an a uniformed policewoman. They advanced towards the guest cottage and the

113

knot of people outside it.

Pleasant looked up at Vera.

" Miz French don't like black people," she said flatly.

" Can't you take the spell off?" Vera panted. " I'll pay you anything you ask."

" For God's sake, shut up!" Justin growled, but it was too late.

" She don't want you to believe me," Pleasant dashed the tears from her eyes. " I knows why. So I isn't covering up for her no more."

" What do you mean, covering up?" Vera shrieked. " Justin, this woman is out to make trouble. Get rid of her!"

The police contingent was only a few yards away from them now and could hear every word. No one but Mel was aware of their presence.

" Justin!" she whispered urgently, but he either did not hear or chose to ignore her.

" Vera, let me handle this," he snapped. " Pleasant, please explain."

Superintendent Marshall had come to a halt and was openly listening. Mel abandoned her attempt to warn the others. It was too late now.

" I don't want to make trouble for no one," said Pleasant, reluctantly, " but if they makes it for me, I says my piece. I isn't the one to put the grave dirt, and isn't the one to threaten to kill Miz Dewar. *You* was, Miz French!"

EIGHT

"Very interesting!" commented Superintendent Marshall, coming forward, and Vera, her face white, gasped. "I'll take the pair of you downtown and we will sort it all out. You have a lot of explaining to do, Mrs. French. Not only this, but why you lied about your movements on the day of the murder." He gestured to his companions. "Take Mrs. French and Mrs. Jackson to the car."

Vera stared at him.

"You can't do this!" she cried, and pulled her arm away from the grasp of the policewoman.

"Please do not resist, or I shall be obliged to arrest you, Madam," he replied coldly. "I came here this morning for the sole purpose of questioning you, but with this new development, that had better take place at the police station."

Vera looked round wildly.

"Justin!"

"Go with the Superintendent, Vera," he said wearily. "Please do not make an undignified fuss. It will merely make matters worse. I will follow you down, and contact Tib."

Vera stumbled away, in the grip of the policewoman.

Justin looked at Aubrey.

"You stay here. Mel, look after him, and don't let him

115

do anything stupid. Gina, you come with me." He started towards the house, then glanced back. "Oh, Mel! When Dominic has finished making arrangements with the mortician, and had his call to New York, ask him to come down to Superintendent Marshall's office."

With that, he was gone, Gina, nothing loath, at his heels.

Mel and Aubrey were left alone by the pool, like a pair of marooned sailors, with nothing to do but look at each other. There was a long, awkward silence. Several times, Mel thought the youth was about to speak, but each time, the words either would not come, or he thought better of them, and looked away, his face troubled. She hoped his worries were for his mother, but that was not inevitable, as his display of heartlessness the other night had shown.

After a while, there was movement round the side of the house. Mel glanced up, to see a stranger approaching. He was tall, very black, and carried himself with an air of great assurance. He was dressed in darkish green denim, which looked vaguely like a uniform, and he wore dark glasses. Aubrey, who had been squatting by the pool, staring into the water, scrambled to his feet.

"Manley!" he cried, as if all his problems were solved.

"I've been looking for you. I heard about your mother," the newcomer replied, but his eyes were on Mel.

She stirred uneasily under the scrutiny of the blank black lenses. So this was Manley, the butler's son, the companion of whom Vera disapproved so strongly. He came as a surprise. She had expected a youth, but this was a man nearer her own age than Aubrey's, a person who knew how to handle himself and whose voice suggested an extensive education.

"You are Miss Grainger," he said. "I have seen you

about the place, but we have not met. I came home only last week, and I do not normally come up to the house. Norman Manley Robertson. Named," he added, with a glimmer of sardonic humour at her ill-concealed astonishment," for one of our National Heroes. You may have heard of him."

Mel gulped. She determined not to be upstaged by him.

"Indeed, I have," she replied coolly, and held out her hand. "How do you do?"

He hesitated fractionally before shaking hands. Mel was satisfied that, for the moment, she had held her own.

"Skip the formalities," muttered Aubrey. "I told you Mel was one of the good guys. Manley, what am I to do about Mom?"

Manley turned his full attention on his young friend.

"Is there anything you should do?"

Aubrey shuffled his feet, embarrassed.

"I guess there might be," he admitted.

"I see. As I have told you before, you are old enough to stand on your own feet, make decisions for yourself, and take the responsibility for them."

Aubrey could not meet Manley's eyes.

"It's not that easy."

"Few things are. Your mother has been taken in for questioning because, apparently, she had lied to the police about her movements on the day of the murder, and also because she was heard to threaten Mrs. Dewar."

Aubrey hunched his shoulders.

"How should I know where she was or what she was doing? I've been trying to keep out of her way since I was sent home. For the first month, she started howling every time she set eyes on me. What with her weeping over me,

117

and Justin lecturing me, and Gina looking down her nose at me, I tell you, man, it's been foul."

"Families are usually upset when someone is sent home from school in disgrace," Manley observed, dispassionately.

"Don't you start!" Aubrey implored him.

"I don't mean to. It was your decision to smoke pot. You knew it was forbidden. You were caught and you have to take the consequences. So, you don't know why your Mother should lie about her movements."

"No," whispered Aubrey, and Mel was sure that it was, at best, no more than half the truth.

She glanced swiftly at Manley. The dark glasses obscured a good deal of his face, but she thought his eyebrows lifted.

"What about the threat to Mrs. Dewar?" he asked. "Did they quarrel?"

Aubrey nodded miserably.

"That Felicity poked her nose into everything. She found out about me and Mom was livid. They had a fight."

"Which Pleasant Jackson overheard when she was collecting the dirty laundry from the bedrooms." Manley paused, then went on, "Aubrey, it won't do. If you will lie to me, you will lie to anyone."

The youth stared at him in stricken silence.

"Your smoking pot and being sacked from school for it isn't enough to account for your mother being in such a rage that she would threaten to kill anyone. Nor for her to lie to the police. The two things must go together somehow. If she is trying to conceal what she was doing on the day of the murder, my guess is that you were the cause of it. Your mother loves you. You may find that love suffocating, but you can't deny it. You know she would do anything to protect you. My guess is that she is doing just that. So

118

what is it that you haven't told me?"

Mel fancied that it was not only mother-love which could be overpowering. A little of Norman Manley Robertson went a very long way. She wished she could see the expression in those hidden eyes.

Aubrey's shoulders sagged.

"They'll send me to prison."

"What have you done?" Manley demanded, sharply.

"I brought a packet of stuff in, when I came home."

"You mean, smuggled?"

"Yes."

"What was it?"

"I didn't ask."

"Pot?"

Aubrey shook his head.

"I guess not. It might have been H."

Manley frowned.

"Heroin? How did you get hold of that?"

"There was a dude at school who was a user. When he heard I was going back to Jamaica, he said I could do him a favour, and get paid for it. I didn't have much choice, man. I owed for the Pot."

"Who else knows about this?"

Aubrey shrugged.

"How should I know? I wasn't such a fool as to tell anyone. Felicity found out. She had a pack of private detectives working for her. The old witch told Mom that she knew, and Mom hit the ceiling."

"What was Felicity doing with private detectives?" Mel chipped in and earned herself an impatient glance from Manley.

"I guess she hired them to get the goods on you and

119

Dominic, and when she found that wouldn't wash, sicked them onto me and Gina. She was looking for a handle to use on Mom. She had a bee in her bonnet about Justin and couldn't bear the thought of Gina sinking her hooks into him. She told Mom she would put the police onto me, if she didn't send Gina away."

"How do you know all this?" Mel demanded.

"Hell! I heard them! Mom's room is next to mine, and they were in there."

"And did your mother threaten Felicity Dewar?" Manley asked sharply.

"I guess she did," Aubrey admitted. "But when Mom is in a temper, she says things she doesn't mean."

"How much of all this does Mr. French know?"

"Only the reason why I was chucked out of school. Mom had to tell him that much."

"And the smuggling?"

"No way!" Aubrey shuddered. "He would have scalped me."

"You know I have to report it?" He glanced at Mel. "I can't cover up, even for him. I work for the National Youth Service. I have been doing special training in Cuba this past year, while this young idiot has been trying to ruin his life in that expensive school in Washington."

Cuba! thought Mel, and recognised that Manley's tailoring model was Fidel Castro. The idea of a youth officer being trained there called up all sorts of notions, and she decided that she had learned a second lesson about the new Jamaica.

"What are you going to do?" she asked.

"I should turn him straight over to the police, but I think we may use an oblique approach. I'll call Lisa Morley.

120

She has connections," he added, and strode off into the house.

He was back in a few minutes.

"We are to go to her house. Will you drive us, Miss Grainger?"

Mel was glad of the excuse. She was determined not to be left out, and Justin had told her to look after his step-brother. Somehow it was important not to fall down on the task. She remembered the rest of his instructions and fled into the house for a word with Dominic.

Aubrey sat in the back of the car, biting his thumb. He spoke only once.

"You don't think Mom could have killed Felicity, do you, Manley?" he asked, unsteadily.

"If you don't know that, how can I tell?" was the discouraging reply.

"No," Mel struck in. "I'm sure she didn't. She really thinks Felicity died because she had grave dirt scattered in her bed. She is terrified."

"She could be putting on an act. She was on the stage, years ago," Manley pointed out.

"No, I'd know if she was," Aubrey said eagerly. "She's real scared."

Manley made a gesture of irritation.

"Superstitious nonsense! And do you believe it, Miss Grainger?"

"I don't know," she replied truthfully. At the back of her mind there lurked the persistent thought that of the four women threatened, two—Felicity and Melissa—were dead. Two down, two to go.

"I would have thought you to have had more sense," he said roughly, then added, ruining his effect, "In any

121

case, my father says it was not done properly. He is certain the dirt came out of one of the flower-beds. Grave dirt should be dug out of a grave opened up specially for the purpose."

"And what is it supposed to do?" Mel inquired, reluctantly curious.

"For those who believe in such things, a power of no good," Manley said shortly. "Nothing specific, just to bring bad luck. Anyone who wished to make sure his enemy died would go to a bit more trouble: have a charm made up, and hung or buried near their house; or knock a rusty nail over the door of their room."

"You have made a study of Obeah?"

"I have no interest in it," Manley rejoined, blightingly. "That is all in the past. I look only to the future."

There speaks Castro's Cuba! thought Mel, and dared probe no further.

The Morleys' house was in a quiet residential district near the Botanical Gardens, everywhere bright with flowering shrubs. Theirs was a white bungalow, on a large plot, screened from its neighbours by a thick flourishing hedge of scarlet Smugglers' Pride. There were two cars on the concrete driveway, large black official-looking vehicles. Mel pulled up behind them.

Lisa came out to meet them, her face grave. She took charge of Aubrey, and led him into the house, while Manley, who clearly knew his way about the place, took Mel through to a shady patio.

"Lisa was with the Narcotics Division, before her marriage," he explained, as they settled themselves in garden chairs. "We can leave this safely to her. But the Law will have to take its course."

122

"What will they do to him? He's only a kid."

"That will be up to the Court."

"Can't you put in a word for him? Isn't there some form of community service he could do instead of going to prison?"

Lisa appeared with a tray on which were glasses of long cold drinks.

"That's the sort of constructive suggestion I go along with," she said. "Manley, surely you could speak to the Resident Magistrate?"

"If the case is settled at that level, maybe," he replied doubtfully.

"You try!" Lisa recommended. "Tib and Justin will be here as soon as they can."

"Who've you got in there?" Manley inquired, with a jerk of his head towards the house.

"My former boss and a couple of his men. And the Custos Rotulorum." She smiled at Mel. "That's a sort of justice of the peace," she explained. "Aubrey may prove very useful, and that will be taken into account."

"He may be even more useful to Miss Grainger and her employer," Manley pointed out. "This opens up a completely new angle on Felicity Dewar's murder. Vera French may have killed her to shut her mouth, but there would be others equally interested in making sure that she could not talk. People who play rough."

Mel snatched at the hope of taking the murder away from the household at Eagles' Nest.

"That must be it!" she exclaimed eagerly.

"Don't count on it," Manley advised, in a dampening tone. "There is, as yet, no evidence that the smugglers knew that Felicity Dewar was on to them. There has been no attack on Aubrey, who is surely the weak link in the chain."

Tib arrived, bringing Justin, both men thoroughly exasperated.

"Vera has clammed up," Tib announced. "She won't say a thing, not to the police, nor to Justin, nor to me. So she is sitting in a detention cell, where she is likely to remain for the whole of Christmas unless she comes to her senses."

"Maybe she will talk when she hears what her son is confessing, this very minute," said Lisa, and the whole sorry tale was related again.

"All that does is provide her with a gold-plated motive," Tib commented. "Superintendent Marshall has sent his minions over to Port Antonio, to try and place Vera there on the day of the murder. She said she was at a big Red Cross meeting in the morning, but no one saw her there, when they should have done, and she arrived very late at a friend's house for a Bridge Party later in the day. She left Eagles' Nest shortly after Felicity herself, and the police reckon she had ample time to drive over to the beach house and back again."

"My family seem to be bent on proving themselves fools," said Justin bitterly. "What will become of Aubrey?"

"I'm being pressured by these ladies to ask for him to be put into my care at the National Youth Service," Manley told him.

"Mel suggested it, and I think it is a very sound idea," said Lisa. "Young offenders merely learn how to become criminals in penal establishments. On the other hand, they can't be allowed to go free."

Justin's eyes rested on Mel.

"I didn't know you were a sociologist," he said, and she

felt the colour fly up into her face.

"I'm sorry," she replied stiffly. "I didn't mean to interfere. It is none of my business."

"Cool it, you two!" Lisa interposed swiftly. "I'll warn the kitchen there will be loads of people here for lunch."

Justin stood up.

"Minus two. Mel and I are going home. There is nothing we can do here. Manley, are you staying?"

"I think I must. To say my piece for Aubrey, if the chance arises."

"We'll leave you the car. Mel can ride back with me."

Given no choice, she followed him out to the driveway, and took her seat in the Mercedes.

"What about Gina?" she asked, as they pulled away from the house.

"Dominic is looking after her. He showed up just as Tib and I were leaving Superintendent Marshall's office."

"What is he doing there?" she asked uneasily.

Justin laughed shortly.

"Not giving himself up, if that is what you are afraid of! Just clearing up a small matter. When he has finished there, I expect he will take Gina to lunch somewhere in town. Gina will hang on for a while to see what happens to Vera, and Dominic has things to do. He had his call to New York. Felicity's Trustee says she is to be cremated here, and the ashes scattered at her estate in Virginia later on. It's a public holiday for the next two days, so the arrangements must be put in hand today. Dominic is going to be very busy," he ended, significantly.

Mel thought she saw the light.

"As you intended he should. You don't mean us to have a moment alone together, do you?"

125

" It's for your own good, believe me. Don't kid yourself into thinking that Superintendent Marshall will write you and Dominic off because of Aubrey and Vera."

126

NINE

Mel woke suddenly. The room was dark, and she wondered how long she had slept. She had lain down on the bed, after lunch, for a short siesta, not even expecting to doze off. That must be hours ago . . .

She reached out and switched on the bedside light. Almost at once, there was a tap on the door, and Lisa Morley looked in.

" You're awake," she said.

Mel struggled onto one elbow, her head still muzzy with sleep.

" What time is it?"

" After eight. Justin said you were not to be woken."

" I must get up."

Lisa perched herself on the edge of the bed.

" There is no great hurry. Dinner is being held back until Vera arrives."

" Is she being released?"

" For the moment. I don't think they want any more prisoners in the cells over Christmas than they can help."

" Christmas!" Mel exclaimed. " I'd forgotten about it. It doesn't feel much like Christmas. What about Aubrey?"

" He's here. That is what I have to talk to you about. There is going to be a very high-level, hush-hush operation, which has already started, and some poor souls are going

127

WOLVERHAMPTON
PUBLIC LIBRARIES

to spend the holiday working. One important part of it is that no word must escape that Aubrey has talked to the police. No one is to know. Not Dominic, or Gina, or even Vera, not until the island has been sewn up so tight that the smugglers can't get out. I have to ask you to give me your promise that you will not say a word."

Mel nodded.

"You have it."

"Good. If the Narcotics Division round up a whole gang of heroin pushers, through Aubrey, it will help his case."

"Will the court listen to Manley?"

Lisa smiled.

"I should be surprised if they did not. He pulls a lot of weight, politically, young though he is. He owes a lot to the French family. Justin's father paid for his education, sent him to a good school, then university. He died while Manley was a freshman, and from then on in Justin picked up the tab."

"And is Manley grateful or is he one of those who bites the hand that feeds him?"

"A year or two back, that might have been the case," Lisa acknowledged. "But he is twenty-four now and he has matured a lot. He allows that Justin is a patriot, even if he doesn't approve of capitalists. He will do his best for Aubrey. You are gathering compliments. Manley says you have sense, and Justin is pleased with you."

Mel felt a great surge of emotion.

"He has a funny way of showing it," she remarked, to cover it.

Lisa laughed.

"Justin is too used to command, and have everyone jump when he speaks. It does him the world of good when

128

you stand up to him." She rose. "Are you going to get dressed now?"

Mel scrambled out of bed.

"I shan't be long."

She had to force herself not to rush, to crush down an idiotic urge to find herself in Justin French's company. She reminded herself sharply that any relationship formed here was strictly a dead end.

No amount of stern reminders could stop her heart missing a beat when he looked up and saw her coming along the terrace, and left his chair to meet her, smiling. Mel wanted to hold out her arms and run to him, despite the presence of the Morleys and Dominic, but Gina and Vera arrived at that moment, and in the ensuing commotion Mel could take time out to regain a grip on herself.

Vera was shattered by the experiences of the day. She collapsed into a chair, complaining of her treatment.

"You should consider yourself fortunate," Justin said grimly. "You might have been locked up all over the holiday. You can't hold out on the police for ever."

Vera looked up at him defiantly.

"What I did and where I was on the day that Felicity was killed is entirely my own affair. It had nothing to do with her. I didn't kill her. I wasn't anywhere near the beach house, and no one can prove that I was."

"That could be true," Tib observed, as he saw Justin's mouth tighten in anger. "Marshall's people haven't turned up a trace of Vera in the vicinity of the beach house on the day of the murder. There was a heavy shower that morning, and the only car tracks deep enough to have been made while the ground was still wet are Felicity's own. The forensic lab. has samples of mud from Vera's tyres, and none

TIT—E 129

of it matches the soil near the beach house. For what it is worth, it looks as though she has been in a sugar-cane field at some time recently. Would you care to comment on that, Vera?"

"No, I would not," she snapped, leaving her chair. " I'm going to have a bath. Where is Aubrey? Out with that Manley, I suppose."

"He's in his room," Justin told her. "He will come down for dinner, when you are ready."

Vera imagined a rebuke, cast her stepson a speaking look and marched into the house.

"I must change, too," said Gina, with a smile only for Justin, and followed her aunt.

"The sooner Vera's house is ready and I can have my home to myself again, the better," he growled, and Mel was obliged to suppress an unworthy hope that the departing Gina might have heard him.

Vera's temper was improved by her bath and a change of clothes, while Gina was ready to dispense sweetness and light, and even a little Christmas spirit, which fell rather flat since no one would respond. Then, shortly after eleven, Justin announced that he was going to Midnight Mass.

"Mel," he added, "are you coming with me?"

Astonishment swept over her, and in the same instant, she became aware that it was shared by everyone in the room.

"Yes," she said, and was annoyed that her voice came out as a squeak. "If you like."

"Get ready then. Five minutes."

Gina recovered herself.

"It would be nice if we all went."

"Do as you please," Justin replied curtly. "Does the

Protestant church have a late service?"

"Oh, no, Gina, I don't think we should go," said Vera hastily, with a worried glance at his face. "I'm too tired."

"Hurry up, Mel," said Justin, ignoring both her and Gina. "It will be packed. We have to be early if we are to find seats."

She fled, not daring to glance back at Gina. When she returned, Justin was alone in lounge.

"They have all gone to bed, and the Morleys have gone home. They asked me to tell you goodnight," he said, and led her out to his waiting car.

"I've never been in a Catholic church," she remarked, a shade nervously, as they drove down into Kingston.

In the darkness, she thought he smiled.

"We don't do anything outstandingly peculiar. I'll tell you when to stand up and sit down. Do you attend your own church?"

"I can't say that I do. Just weddings—and funerals," she added, as the past rushed back on her suddenly.

"You have never felt the need for religion?"

She hesitated. It was a topsy-turvy situation, to be sitting in a car with this man, in the middle of the night, involved with murder and drugs, discussing a topic she would normally shy from. Yet it was a moment for confidences.

"At times," she admitted, and knew that she had to tell him something of her real self, not her assumed identity. "I looked after my parents. My father had a stroke, and the nursing gave my mother a heart attack. She died, and I had to take over. Dad was shattered. He couldn't believe that she had gone first. He made up his mind to follow her. It took him over a year. Then he had another stroke, and he didn't recover. In all those months, I often wished that I knew how or whom to pray to."

"And I thought you were a hard little piece who cared only for Number One," Justin said softly. "I began to suspect I was wrong a day or two ago. Now I know it. Have you a prejudice against Catholics?"

"I don't think so," she said cautiously.

Justin laughed.

"Your honesty is refreshing. I should tell you that there was a girl once, years ago, when I was a student. We had something going, it came to an end and she blamed my religion. It wasn't that, but she had prejudices. The truth was that we both wanted different things. I used to play tennis, in those days. She wanted me to win Wimbledon for her. My ambition was to follow my father in the business, here in Jamaica. That taught me a lesson, Mel. People have to be taken for what they are. I am what I am. You are what you are. Can we accept that, you and I?"

Mel's heart lurched. Without the slightest warning, she had come to a moment of truth. She knew that she should do one of two things: either say 'No', or confess to her real identity. Neither was possible. It was already too late for confessions, and she could not bring herself to choke him off.

"I wish we could," she said, in a low voice.

They drove on in silence for a little while.

"What's past is past," he said, at last. "That goes for both of us." He turned into the church car park. "I'm not trying to rush you, Mel. You have enough on your mind without my adding to it, but when all this is over, we shall have things to say to each other."

If only you knew! she thought, and allowed him to take her into the church.

It was like dropping out of time. For an hour or more, she forgot the trap in which she was caught, the menace of the future, the sorrows of the past, the horrors of the present. She was one of a hot mass of happy people, all dressed up to the nines, so that she wished she possessed a hat and gloves like the other women. Lights, music and a whiff of incense—it was all strange, yet friendly, and for the first time since she arrived on the island, it did not seem inappropriate to sing the carols she had learnt in childhood. It was Christmas, after all.

They drove back through the warm, scented night. Eagles' Nest was in darkness, save for a few lights left burning to guide their steps. They parted on the terrace.

"Goodnight, Mel," said Justin, and for a breathless moment, she thought he was going to kiss her, but he did not. He stepped back. "Sleep well," he added abruptly, and turned away.

She went to her room, her mind in turmoil. She thought of home, of the people she had crossed the Atlantic to dodge. Helen and Scott, once best friend and first and only love. She discovered that all resentment was gone. She no longer cared that Scott had jilted her. He had done her a favour. She would never have been happy with him. He had tried to do the thing which Justin condemned: change her, make her turn from the course she had thought right. Over the long miles which separated her from Scott and his wife, she sent them a mental festive greeting.

The Christmas spirit was noticeably lacking the next morning. Gifts were exchanged. Mel trotted out the collection of small gaily wrapped packages she found in her bedroom, each labelled in Melissa's handwriting, and was thankful that her sister had had the forethought to prepare

133

them. In return, she received things bought for her vanished twin, and could hardly bring herself to open them. For her there was no pleasure in either the giving or receiving, and she had a strong impression that she was not alone in that feeling.

Seasonal fare was laid out on a buffet beside the pool at lunchtime, while Vera moaned at the necessity of putting off the guests they had invited.

"You could be in the cells," Dominic reminded her, and provoked an outburst.

The hours dragged past. Mel spent her time by the pool, swimming or reading, while from the sitting-room of the cottage came the steady rattle of the typewriter. Christmas Day or not, Dominic felt like working. Mel asked if she could help and was shooed out.

Justin sat on the terrace of the house, apparently reading, but each time that Mel looked across at him, his eyes were on her. Gina occupied a chair near him and watched them both.

There was a party for the servants that night. Although their quarters were built at the far side of the garden, sounds of music and laughter drifted across on the evening breeze. It was nice, thought Mel, standing on the verandah outside her room listening, to know that some people were enjoying themselves. The dreary party in the house had broken up early, to leave the staff free.

Gina came round the side of the pool.

"I want a word with you, Mel. Shall we go into your room?"

Mel could imagine what was coming.

"If you like," she said evenly.

"Now," said Gina, putting her back to the door, as soon

134

as they were inside. "I warned you, didn't I? And you have taken no notice. Did you think I was bluffing?"

"It is a matter of indifference to me whether you were bluffing or not. I was at the conference all day, and so you could not have seen me on the Port Antonio road. If you go telling that story to the police, mightn't they want to know how it is that you were there and not shopping in Kingston as you said you were?"

Gina tossed her head scornfully.

"They won't give me a second thought once they have you handed to them on a plate. I know what conferences are like. People come and go. No one can swear that any other person was there all the time. You have been clever, Mel, but not clever enough."

Someone banged on the door.

"Gina? Are you in there?" came Vera's agitated voice.

"Let her in," Mel recommended, and Gina, startled, did so.

Vera was in her dressing-gown, her hair dishevelled as if she had just risen.

"I thought you had gone to bed," Gina said.

"I had. Only I couldn't sleep and I thought you might have an aspirin. When I found your room empty, I knew you must be here. What are you trying to do?"

Gina's mouth set into a thin line.

"What I told you I would do."

Vera sighed.

"Didn't you listen to me at all? If Justin doesn't want you, there is nothing you can do to make him."

"I'm not losing him to Mel."

"You can't lose what you never had," Vera snapped, in a burst of sense of which Mel had not thought her capable.

135

" Justin has never given you a moment's encouragement. The only person who thought you could catch him was Felicity—"

The colour flared in Gina's face, and her carefully composed veneer of assurance cracked.

" Auntie Vee," she cut in, " I'm not going to be cheated again. What do you think I am? A born loser?"

Vera shook her head.

" Of course, you are not a loser. A couple of disappointments are nothing, at your age."

"They are something to me!" Gina cried, and flung back the door. "Mel needn't think she can get away with this. She knows I can stop her, and I will!"

She ran out of the room, tears streaming down her face.

" What did she mean: she would not be cheated again?" Mel asked.

Vera dragged a hand through her hair.

" She got let down badly last year, poor kid. She doesn't know much about men—yet. She's learning." She trailed over to the door. " I suppose you will tell Justin?"

Mel recognised a veiled appeal.

" Not unless I have to."

Vera rewarded her with a tired smile.

" You are kinder than we deserve. I'm sorry I haven't made you more welcome." She hesitated, then went on, " Can Gina make trouble for you?"

" Possibly."

" Justin won't thank her if she does. I'll try to stop her. She's upset now, but she might listen to me in the morning. Goodnight."

Mel strolled out onto the verandah, to watch Vera go back into the house. She smelt tobacco and turned to see Dominic in the doorway of the sitting-room, smoking a cigarette.

"What was all that about?"

"Gina is threatening to blow the whistle on us."

"I shouldn't let it worry you," he said calmly. "As long as the police haven't found Melissa, we can claim mistaken identity. Your alibi is iron-clad. After all, Port Antonio is on the other side of the island. You couldn't have nipped out of the conference for half an hour, driven over there, killed Felicity and been back again for the coffee break."

Mel wished she shared his confidence. Once the police picked up Melissa's trail, they would have plenty of witnesses to swear she was on the north coast on the day of the murder. Mrs. Nelson and the receptionist at the Planters' Inn knew Melissa too well to be written off as mistaken.

"Vera has promised to talk her out of it, if she can."

Dominic pulled a face.

"Bully for her! A few hours in the cells must have worked wonders." He yawned. "I think I'll turn in. Good-night."

Mel went to her own bed, much depressed. What a way to have spent Christmas Day! Then it came to her why the hours seemed to have been wasted: with Gina hovering like a vulture, Justin had not had a chance to exchange more than a few words with her.

That does it! she thought. You've fallen for a man you deceived and on whose hospitality you have imposed. A proud man, who might not readily forgive . . .

In the morning, he came to share breakfast with her, and her joy swamped her misgivings.

"I suggest we go out today," he said. "Anywhere. Just to get away from this house and my womenfolk. I never had you to myself for a moment, yesterday. Felicity's Trustee

137

will be arriving this evening. We shall have to be back to receive him. And then, tomorrow, the whole business will start up again, and no doubt the police will be all over us once more. That Irish cousin will be coming, too. So today is our last chance of freedom. Let's go straight away, before the others are up. We don't want them either trying to stop us or wanting to come with us."

"Are you still aiming to keep me from conspiring with your cousin?" she asked slyly.

He grinned back at her.

"You catch on quickly, young lady! Now, go and get ready. You know I'm an impatient man, and I don't like being kept waiting."

Mel fled into her room, and flung open her wardrobe door intent on fetching out Melissa's prettiest dress to replace the shorts and shirt she had put on that morning. She changed quickly, then hunted for a smarter pair of sandals among the shoes stored under the hanging clothes. Her hand touched something soft and slightly damp.

It was right at the back of the wardrobe, in a corner and it felt like vegetation . . .

She fell to her knees, pushing back the garments on the hangers to give her a clear view.

It was a bundle, neatly tied up in string. A package, wrapped in large green leaves, still moist and fresh, open at each end. She peered inside, and identified sticks, feathers, eggshells and a fishbone.

She had never seen anything like it before in her life, but she did not need telling what it was.

It had to be an Obeah charm.

She opened her mouth and screamed.

TEN

Somewhere, a long way off, a dry professional voice was saying,

". . . I am not familiar with the circumstances of the case, but I would say that Miss Grainger has been under considerable strain for a prolonged period. I have observed like symptoms in persons who have spent months nursing relatives, or who have had a series of deaths in the family . . ."

Mel opened one eye cautiously. She had no idea where she was, and no recollection of anything beyond the discovery of that horrible thing in the wardrobe and people rushing in when she screamed. She opened the other eye and looked round. She was in a strange room: large, beautifully furnished, with Venetian blinds half-closed against the bright light outside. A little black nurse sat in a chair in one corner, leafing through the pages of a magazine. In the middle of the wall opposite the bed was an open door leading to another room. The voice was coming from there.

". . . As I told you yesterday, the shock is disproportionate to the immediate cause . . ."

Yesterday? Had she lost a whole day?

". . . And none of you had noticed anything unusual?"

"She fell asleep, the other day, and was out for hours."

That was Dominic.

"All to the good." The professional voice again, obviously a doctor. "The body trying to find its own best remedy. Normally I would recommend several weeks of rest and complete quiet, but I realise that, in the present circumstances, it is impossible. The police cannot be impeded in their investigation."

"The Coroner co-operated. He waived her evidence."

Justin's voice, and the knowledge that he was so near brought intense pleasure. She tried to sit up, and at once the nurse was at the bedside, arranging the pillows to prop her up. Then she slipped in to the adjoining room, to reappear with the doctor. Behind them came Justin and Dominic, but the nurse drove them out again.

The doctor was a large, elderly man, black with a distinct hint of Chinese.

"We will soon have you on your feet again," he said reassuringly. "We had to give you a sedative yesterday, but that wore off hours ago, and you have been sleeping normally. I shall leave you some tablets, and I shall want to see you at my office in a week's time. I suggest you rest in bed until late afternoon, then you may get up if you feel like it."

Justin and Dominic came in, briefly, after the doctor had gone, to hover in typically awkward male uneasiness in the face of sickness.

"I'm all right," she told them. "I'm sorry to have put everyone to so much trouble. I feel a complete fool."

Vera came, and even Gina, looking sulky. But no police and Mel concluded that Vera must have succeeded in persuading her niece to keep quiet. She wondered how long it would last. Gina bore a marked resemblance to a time bomb, ticking away.

140

Four o'clock struck, somewhere in the house, and the nurse, who for all her diminutive size, was a proper tyrant, permitted her to get up, informing her that she would be leaving but would return immediately if required. Mel thanked her and went down. She had not been on the upper levels of the house before, but she had been lodged in the best bedroom, at the head of the main staircase and so she had no difficulty in finding her way.

There was no one in the lounge, but it was the usual hour for tea to be served on the terrace. They were all there, and with them two strangers. Justin jumped up when he caught sight of her, and appeared to be under the impression that she could not stand without the aid of his arm. Mel leant gratefully, giving in to temptation.

Introductions were made.

" Mr. Wartburg, Felicity's Trustee, and sort of honorary uncle," Justin said, with more than a little malice in his voice.

Wilmot S. Wartburg offered a thin dry hand. He was withered with age, but his eye was bright. He emanated a lively air of malignance.

" And Mr. O'Donnell, Felicity's distant cousin," Justin went on, when she had exchanged meaningless pleasantries with the old man.

Mel found herself looking into a pointed, smiling face, slightly below the level of her own.

" Philip James, but everyone calls me P.J. You don't want to be formal, do you?"

The voice was light and charming, the Irish accent soft. P.J. was a young leprechaun, fine-boned, brown-haired, with blue eyes which danced with fun. It might not be the grave demeanour suitable to one arrived for a funeral, but the joyous spirit bubbled up irrepressibly.

He talked incessantly, amusingly, lightening the atmosphere, and even bringing a twitch to the pinched mouth of Mr. Wartburg.

But as soon as he could, Justin drew Mel away from the others, and into the garden. As with the design of the house, so whoever had laid out the grounds had taken advantage of the hillside and built a series of terraces descending to the perimeter fence. They strolled down through the bright flowers, tall Poinsettias like giant cousins of the poor little pot plants she had seen at home, cascades of pink and white bougainvillea, yellow Alamander, and trees such as she had never seen.

"My mother created this garden," Justin told her. "There wasn't the smallest plant put in except under her direction. She loved this place."

Mel looked round her.

"Not surprising. Who wouldn't love it?"

He put his hands on her shoulders and turned her gently to face him.

"Mel, you had me worried yesterday. You passed out at my feet. The doctor says you have been under strain for quite a time. Is that so?"

There was barely a couple of inches difference in height between them. She had only to raise her eyes a fraction to look into his. What she saw made her heart turn over.

"It could be," she admitted, summoning up courage to spill the whole truth to him.

He misread her hesitation.

"I'm sorry. I promised myself I wouldn't try to force your confidence. Understand this: whatever you have been involved in, it is all in the past now. Finished. Over and

142

done with."

She felt the tears start into her eyes.

" I wish it were," she whispered.

" My darling, don't cry!" he exclaimed, and put his arms round her.

No one had ever kissed her like that before. It was a whole new experience, the gateway into an enchanted world. She gave herself up to his embrace, and his arms tightened round her, as mutual delight kindled a fiery furnace.

Dominic surprised them.

" Sorry! I can see I am interrupting," he said, his eyes alive with interest. " You know, it never occurred to me that you two might get something going."

Reluctantly, Justin released Mel.

" What do you want?"

" Escape from Wilmot S. Wartburg, for starters. Did you know that old fink has come complete with dossiers from Felicity's private eye, to hand over to Superintendent Marshall?"

" He would!" Justin commented.

" You and he seem to have got across each other remarkably, on the strength of one day's acquaintance," Dominic remarked. " Really, I came to talk to Mel."

" Ready to confess?" Justin inquired.

Mel started. Confess what?

" Right on!" said Dominic sheepishly. " You made me say my piece to the Superintendent, and I have offered my apologies to Vera, who did not receive them very kindly, I might add. Mel's turn now."

" My turn for what?"

" Dominic is working round to telling you that he was responsible for the grave dirt. To see how you all would react," Justin said sardonically. " He has an insatiable curiosity about the vagaries of human behaviour. He experiments on people."

"Then that soil wasn't out of a grave?"

"I dug it out of the garden," Dominic admitted.

Mel was conscious of a huge wave of relief, which she would have died rather than admit in front of these two. Modern young women ought not to be frightened by ancient superstitions.

"Then that parcel in my wardrobe—" she began, then stopped short for Dominic was shaking his head.

"That was the real thing," Justin said quietly. " But not to bring you harm, my darling. That charm was put there to protect you. In case whoever scattered the grave dirt had inadvertently called up something evil. The fact that Felicity died violently so soon after raised all sorts of primitive fears in my staff—and in my family," he added with a smile.

"To protect me? That thing?"

"I agree that it did look rather fearsome, and it is true that the same ingredients are used for both sorts of charm, but I have it on the best authority that your parcel was to protect you. It wasn't intended for you to find it."

She stared at him.

"You mean, there is someone here, in this house, a witch-doctor, or whatever? An Obeahman?"

"No. Obeah is strictly to do harm. A black art. But it has a white counterpart, Myalism, which aims only to do good. Both go back to the religion of the Gold Coast, where the bulk of the slaves came from. In Ashanti there were wizards, the Obayifo, and their enemies the priests, the Okomfo. There were men of both sorts among the slaves, and once they were here, the British authorities couldn't

144

or wouldn't distinguish between them. They were obliged to go underground, and became Obeah and Myalism. The Myalmen often had a rough time. They were confused with the Obeahmen, and after the Slave Trade was stopped there were no new priests coming from Africa. They survived by adapting themselves. The practices of certain Christian sects betray Myalist origins."

"And one of the servants is a Myalman? Who?"

"George. You must have noticed that eye of his. Both Obeah and Myal men are known as ' four-eyed ' because it is supposed they have the power of seeing and talking to spirits. Part of the training seems to consist of staring at the sun when they are children. Hence the defective vision."

"And do they talk to spirits?"

"Who knows? They certainly have heightened perceptions and George has considerable powers of telepathy. Don't be afraid of him, Mel. He is a Native Baptist and a very upright man."

And one to be trusted. She was sure, now, that he knew who she was—and he had said nothing.

"It was kind of him to wish to protect me."

Justin took her hand in his.

"He knew I was in love with you before I knew it myself."

"And is he protecting you too?"

"Oh, Justin doesn't need it," Dominic broke in. "There's a saying: ' French Obi, him strongest ' " he added, in a comic accent, rolling his eyes in mock fear.

Mel was forced to laugh.

"And what does that mean?"

"Nothing to do with my family," Justin replied. "Obeahmen have always feared the Christian Church, es-

145

pecially the French Catholic priests with whom they came in contact in the West Indies. They found it a stronger Obi than their own. There was a frightful bandit called Three Fingered Jack, sometime in the eighteenth century, who thought he could never be caught because he had an Obeah charm. It was a goat's horn filled with ashes, grave dirt, and human fat mixed with the blood of a black cat. It was a Christian who got him eventually."

Mel shivered.

"It's all horrible." A thought struck her, and she turned to Dominic. "While you are in a confessing mood, was it you who put that extra chair at the table the day we found Felicity?"

"Afraid so!"

"And your own wife lately dead! Why, for goodness sake?"

"To see what would happen. I can't expect you to understand, any of you, but this whole thing seems to be happening to somebody else half the time. I'm in it, but I'm watching it all, too. Taking notes, probing, trying experiments. I know it sounds callous, but someday I shall be using all this experience. Writers aren't always very nice people, you know," he added, apologetically.

"No," Justin agreed. "Now go away. It will be dark soon, and I suppose I shall have to spend the evening playing the good host to that frightful Wartburg. I want a bit of time with Mel. So, scoot!"

This is the moment, she thought, when I must tell him who I am. The deception cannot go on any longer.

Dominic was half-way up the steps leading back to the next terrace and eventually to the house when one of the maids appeared higher up, calling to him. He looked up,

146

exchanged a word with her, then started back down.

"Mel! Telephone for you!"

Behind her she heard Justin swear under his breath.

"I had better go," she said awkwardly, wondering who it could be. A painful hope shot into her mind. Was it possible that Melissa was not dead, and was waiting at the other end of the line to explain why she had not returned sooner? The idea sent her racing up the garden, careless that her breakneck haste might look, to Justin, like flight.

But it was not Melissa. A Jamaican voice floated over the wire.

"This is Mrs. Nelson."

"Oh, yes," Mel said, deflated. "Has Peter turned up?"

It could be important, but in the acuteness of her disappointment, she thought nothing of it.

"No, he has not. I've loved that no-good bum like my own son, and he didn't come back for his Christmas dinner. I thought you might have seen him."

"No, he's not around here. Not to my knowledge. I'm sorry."

"It's the last time I'll buy a turkey and all the trimmings for him," said Mrs. Nelson, aggrieved. "Call me if he shows up, will you, honey?"

Mel promised and hung up. The house was quiet, no one in the lounge, or on the terrace. She supposed that most of them had gone to their rooms to change for the evening. Hopefully, she ran down the garden as the brief tropical dusk descended, but Justin was gone. With lagging steps she returned to the house.

She went up to her new room. All her things had been moved in there, so clearly she was meant to keep it. She gave a thought to her bedroom back home. It would fit into

147

one corner of this one. It was going to feel very pockey. It was all too easy, she had discovered, to accustom oneself to the trappings of wealth.

There was no hope of a private word with Justin. He was an excellent host, attentive to all his guests, and he made no move to single her out after dinner, though often she caught his eyes resting on her. But the old uncertainty was back in his face: there were even flashes of suspicion every time Dominic addressed her. Wretchedly, she told herself that it was just as well.

Justin was not the only one to watch her. Gina was there, and not at all her normal self. She did not put herself forward, making up to Justin, as was her habit, but sat quietly, hardly taking part in the conversation. There was an expression of self-satisfaction on her face which made Mel's flesh creep. She wondered if Gina had seen her with Justin in the garden. If she had, Mel was sure her promise of silence would be thrown to the winds. Gina would be out for revenge. And there was nothing to be done about it, except wait for the blow to fall.

The evening would have been trying but for P. J. O'Donnell. Atmospheres meant nothing to him, and he entertained them all, in an inconsequential way. All the same, it was a relief when certain members of the party decided to have an early night. Aubrey, as out of harmony with his elders as usual, had disappeared straight after dinner, to his own room, since he was forbidden by the police to leave the house. Mr. Wartburg dallied with coffee and brandy for an hour, then went to bed. Vera and Gina retired half an hour later.

"Cheerful bunch, aren't they?" said P.J. in a low voice to Mel who was sharing one of the long settees with him.

148

"How do you manage to live in this morgue?"

She smiled.

"I didn't know you'd noticed."

"What it's like?" he grinned back at her. "Do me a favour! I'm not that stupid. This place gives me the screaming horrors. If I never stop talking it's because I'm overcome with embarrassment."

"You? never!"

"It's the holy all of it! My Ma and her overdeveloped sense of family obligations!"

"What's that?"

"She got me into all this," P.J. confided. "I nearly had a fit when I read her cable."

"Then why did you come?"

"I've a habit of obedience. A very strong-minded woman, my Ma. I'll not be standing up to her, even when she's thousands of miles away. But, you know, I'm perfectly well aware that Felicity wouldn't want one of us even at her funeral."

"No? It's a courtesy."

"Ah, but she didn't want to have anything to do with us. I expect she thought we were peasants, living in a pig sty, and only thinking of standing there with our hands held out for donations from our rich American cousins. Ma was very touched by the letter that Dominic wrote after the old man died, but I'll bet that Felicity didn't know a thing about it. Did she?"

"No," Mel admitted. "Dominic thought she was very rude, trying to snub your mother."

"There you are, then," said P.J. triumphantly. "Ma's a stickler for doing things right, and since I was loafing about Antigua, I'm lumbered. It's a judgement on me, of course."

Mel laughed.

"What for? What have you done?"

"Oh, I'm the black sheep of the family presently," he said, his eyes full of mischief. "I was supposed to follow in my Da's footsteps and take to the Law, the Saints preserve us! I've been grinding away at university for three years and I flunked the finals, last June. The parents were very upset. The only one who was half-way decent was my uncle Stephen and he is dying of the drink, poor man."

"What are you doing in Antigua? Cramming?"

"The divil a bit! I'll have to go back soon, and be an articled clerk in my father's office, but for the moment I'm free. I have a friend, David Astley, who lives on Antigua and he happened to be in England collecting a new boat when the doom fell on me. I crewed for him across the Atlantic and I've been lending a hand in the marina he runs, and helping with some of the charters, in return for my keep."

"Sounds fun," Mel commented, a shade wistfully. She envied those who could jack up everything and take themselves off to some far corner of the world.

"I had a bit of money in my sock," P.J. confided. "Legacy from my grandmother. And Uncle Stephen sends me subs. I'm his heir, anyway, and he hasn't much longer to go. In fact, when that cable arrived from Ma, I thought it would be to say he had gone. I'll miss him, when he does. I've been thinking I should go back to Ireland or I'll be too late to see him again," he added, in as sober a tone as was possible in one so lively.

Justin was sitting in an armchair, reading a newspaper. Dominic, who had been prowling restlessly about the room, came to a halt in front of him.

"We have got off fairly lightly, so far," he remarked. "There hasn't been much in *The Gleaner* about Felicity."

His cousin looked up.

"You wait until tomorrow's issue," he said grimly. "Didn't you notice the reporters at the inquest this morning? They were lapping it up. We shall be spread all over the front page tomorrow, an editorial godsend at a time when there is not much news."

"Much good may it do them," Dominic muttered, and ambled over to stand before Mel.

"What was that phone call? Anything interesting?"

She would have preferred not to discuss it in front of P.J., but Dominic did not appear to mind.

"Mrs. Nelson. Peter Power hasn't shown up yet."

Justin laid aside his newspaper.

"Then he has gone. One way or the other. Either finished off by the assassin if he was with Felicity when she was killed, or off the island and away free because he is the murderer."

"He left most of his gear behind," Mel objected. "Valuable things by the look of it. Cameras."

"A blind to cover his escape," Justin said. "When you think about it, he was the obvious person to take Felicity scuba diving. All that underwater photography. She would think nothing of him taking a spear along on a trip."

"It was your spear."

"Another blind, to cast suspicion on any one of us who happened to be without an alibi."

"Do let me in on this," P.J. broke in eagerly. "Do you know who did it?"

"We have our suspicions," Justin replied. "Felicity had a boy friend on the north coast. We think it was a photog-

151

rapher by the name of Peter Power. He could have killed
her. The main snag is that there is not visible motive. It was
in his interest to keep her alive. She was all set to divorce
Dominic and lay her considerable wealth at his feet."

P.J.'s merry face clouded.

" Power, did you say? That's a good old Irish name. I've
some cousins called Power." He stopped suddenly. " Oh,
my God!" he exclaimed, and there was not a vestige of
levity in his voice. " I can give you a motive."

" What for?" Justin demanded.

" Felicity's murder. It's wild, but its possible. You've
heard about the Farrell Trust, the way Felicity's father tied
up her inheritance? Obviously you have, but do you know its
terms? I had a long session with Mr. Wartburg this morning, because it seems that the Farrell bread is all coming
back to Ireland. It will be shared between my mother and
her brother and another cousin. People have committed
murder for a lot less than a third share in upwards of twenty
million dollars. Mr. Wartburg didn't tell me the name of the
other heir, but suppose it is Power?"

" And is this cousin of yours a photographer?" Justin
inquired.

P.J. shrugged.

" Search me! We don't know that branch of the family.
Our grandmothers fell out at a funeral forty years ago."

" There must be some way of finding out," Dominic put
in eagerly.

P.J., back to his normal self, grinned.

" Easy. Just ask old Wartburg."

Dominic let out a snort of disgust.

" He wouldn't tell me the time of day!"

" He will tell the police anything they want," Justin

pointed out. "They are the ones to handle this. I'll speak to the Superintendent in the morning. If you are right, P.J., they will soon trace Peter Power." He looked at Mel. "It's late and you are supposed to be resting. If you don't go to bed soon, I shall have to send for that nurse again. And don't forget to take one of those pills. You need a good night's sleep."

She felt she was being dismissed. But it was true that she was tired. She did as she was bidden. As she closed the door of the lounge behind her, she heard Justin say,

"We shall have to try and keep the press away from her."

The words were like cold water flung in her face. If Peter Power were the murderer, no one would have the smallest interest in her. Didn't Justin believe that he was?

And as for Justin himself, desolately she wondered if they could ever reach an understanding. That day she had discovered that he loved her, that her own dreams were not mere shadows, but could the new-found feeling withstand the shocks which were bound to come? If only she had told him! So many times, she had felt the urge to confide, but always she had held back. It would have to be done tomorrow, first thing. He was too precious now to risk losing.

But in the morning, there was only Dominic on the verandah of the guest cottage, eating a solitary breakfast. Mel joined him.

"Where is everybody?"

Dominic looked up from the morning paper. Justin had been right: *The Gleaner* had gone to town on them. There was a horrible fascination in reading it.

"Vera and Gina never get up, and that Wartburg is

153

having a tray in his room, the Lord be praised. Justin has gone to his office and he has taken young P.J. with him, to air his theory to Superintendent Marshall. The funeral is at noon, but Justin thinks you shouldn't attend. Vera and Gina won't be going, either. It will be a purely male contingent, to withstand the assaults of the news hounds."

So the explanations would have to be postponed. Mel could have cried with impatience.

Dominic set aside the newspaper. There was a little pile of mail on the table. From it, he picked up a large envelope bearing English stamps.

" This is addressed to Felicity, but I may as well open it. It looks like a catalogue or something." He drew out a slim glossy brochure. " What do you know? Felicity fancied a boat. Look, Mel, it's the Tradewind. She must have taken notice of Melissa's ravings about Jim's boat."

Mel peered over his shoulder as he leafed through the brochure. She knew nothing about sailing, but that yacht was so beautiful that she no longer wondered that her sister was keen to cruise on it. It was tragic to think of it wrecked and broken.

" I wouldn't mind having one of these, if I had twenty-seven thousand pounds handy," said Dominic. " How much is that in dollars? We shan't have much difficulty tracking this, when we are free to look for Melissa. My uncle would have been mad about it. He was a keen sailor. He had Justin in a boat before he could toddle. And me, too, when I was shunted over here. The last few years of his life, when Justin was more or less running the business alone, he and Vera spent most of their time cruising."

" Doesn't Justin keep a boat now?"

" Only that dinghy at the beach house. He works too hard

to spare time for sailing." He broke off, raising his head, listening. "What's going on?"

Mel became aware of noises. Shouts, running feet, then a woman screaming. She looked round but could see nothing.

"Down the garden," said Dominic, identifying the direction of the commotion. "Come on!"

They had gone no more than twenty yards when a dishevelled figure appeared, running towards them. It was Vera, in her dressing-gown, her hair and eyes wild. Tears were streaming down her cheeks. She stopped short when she caught sight of them. They ran towards her.

"What's happened?" Dominic shouted.

Vera flung herself at Mel, clawed fingers tearing at her hair and face.

"Why did you have to do it?" she screamed. "Gina was satisfied with the money. She wouldn't have been on your back for ever. Why did you have to kill her?"

ELEVEN

The police had commandeered Justin's study once more. Mel sat before her interrogator and prepared herself for the worst.

Superintendent Marshall said quietly,

" Miss Grainger, I want you to understand the nature of the accusations which Mrs. French is making against you. She claims that Gina Rawlings told her that she could break your alibi for the day on which Felicity Dewar was murdered; that there was bad blood between you and Miss Rawlings over the affections of Mr. Justin French; and that Miss Rawlings had suddenly decided to take a long trip to Europe. She did not possess that sort of money, and, when pressed, informed her aunt that a satisfactory financial arrangement had been reached."

" Not with me," Mel put in swiftly. " I don't have that sort of money either."

" Mr. Dominic Dewar has. Or will have, once his wife's Will has been proved. As I expect you know, her capital was tied up in a Trust, but she had personal property amounting to several hundred thousand dollars, and the Will which she made at the time of her marriage to Mr. Dewar is still valid. According to Mr. Wartburg, who is her lawyer as well as her trustee, Mrs. Dewar was hoping to obtain a divorce and had mentioned to him that a new

156

Will would be required as soon as she had remarried. But she died before any of that could take place, and Mr. Dewar will be in a position to buy himself anything he wishes. Including silence."

Mel took a grip on herself. Once again, she was haunted by the thought that, perhaps, both she and Melissa had been used—as unwitting accessories to murder.

"To proceed with Mrs. French's accusations: she is of the opinion that Miss Rawlings was blackmailing you and Mr. Dewar, and that one or other of you killed her because you feared that she would come back again and again, demanding more money."

Mel said nothing. Feeble protestations of innocence would cut no ice.

"You have been warned that anything you say will be taken down and may be used against you," the Superintendent went on, in the same bland tone. "And you may think it wise to say nothing until your legal advisor, Mr. Morley, is here, but I would suggest that you consider carefully your position. Gina Rawlings was killed some time last night. Late evening seems most likely, since she was fully dressed and her bed had not been slept in. She was found at the lowest terrace of the garden, by the perimeter fence. She would not be likely to wander so far from the house in the dark unless she was meeting someone. She was killed by several blows on the head from a large stone. It appears she was taken unawares, being struck from behind. Unfortunately, the surface of the stone will not reveal finger-prints, but there may be spots of blood on the murderer's clothes. Every stitch of clothing in this house will be examined. This murder was committed by someone who slept here last night. There is a high perimeter fence, patrolled

157

by a watchman, and there are no signs of attempted entry by an intruder." He paused, then added," you may wonder why I am being so frank."

"No doubt you have your reasons," she said cautiously, as he was waiting for a reply.

"Indeed, I have. I want to help you, Miss Grainger. It seems to me that you have landed yourself in a mess. If you have conspired with Dominic Dewar in the murder of his wife, I fail to see what you now stand to gain from it. Not marriage with him, since it appears you prefer Mr. French, who is a very rich man, so there is no financial motive, either. So what was it? Hatred for an overbearing woman? Or were you sorry for him? I'm told she stifled his talent. Whatever the reason, I feel sure that the murder of Gina Rawlings puts a different complexion on the matter, but whether you connived at that or not, you are liable to be charged as an accessory. Think it over, Miss Grainger. Talk it over with your lawyer. Your best interest lies in making a full statement, in naming the accomplice who committed the actual murder at the beach house. It is your only hope of a reduced sentence."

There was a terrifying silence, broken by the shrill ringing of the telephone.

"Yes," said Marshall into it, irritated by the interruption. "What? . . . Oh, yes, very well. I'll come straight over." He replaced the handset, and turned his eyes on Mel. "I have to go. Think it over, Miss Grainger."

Relief that she was not actually under arrest made her weak. With trembling knees she made her way into the lounge.

Aubrey was there, stretched full length on a settee.

"Where's Dominic?" she demanded.

"Gone to the funeral."

"The police let him go? Oh, yes, I suppose they would have to. It isn't as though he can get away. None of us can. This is an island. Aubrey, *could* Dominic have killed Gina?"

"Any of us could," he replied airily. "We were all in separate bedrooms. Unless you and Justin slept together."

Mel's face flamed.

"No, you horrible boy!"

"I didn't think so," he grinned, unabashed. "Justin is much too proper. No sex outside marriage for him, if you can credit it in this day and age! I hope you know what you are doing, taking on Justin. He's a devout son of the Church. I expect you'll have a great gang of kids."

To a bereaved orphan, it sounded like Paradise, and about as remote. The inside of a Jamaican prison was a much more likely future. Sheer terror at the prospect threatened to suspend her thinking processes. She made a great effort of will to consider the position with some calm.

"I wonder who did kill Gina."

"It's knocked my theory on the head."

"What theory?"

"About who killed Felicity. I had Gina pegged for that."

Mel stared.

"But Gina hardly knew Felicity."

"Is that so?" Aubrey shook his head. "You don't want to believe everything people tell you, especially when there has been a murder in the family. Felicity had it in for Gina —and she wasn't the sort of woman to do nothing about it. It was all go, with her. Gina had a murky past and Felicity's private dick turned it up."

Mel collapsed into a chair.

"Well, for goodness sake! What was it?"

" Gina was up to her neck in a stinking divorce case last year. Co-respondent, no less. She was working as a doctor's receptionist in Boston, then, and the man involved was her boss. One of the Founding Families, you know. Descendent of the Pilgrim Fathers and all that jazz. Gina thought she was onto a good thing, but he was only using her to get rid of his wife. He married a rich patient as soon as the divorce was over. Gina came home, and set her sights on Justin. The last thing in the world that she wanted was for him to find out about Boston."

" And Felicity threatened to tell him?"

" I guess so. But she under-estimated Gina. They were two of a kind. She spied on Felicity, and when she discovered the boy friend, hired a guy to take photographs so that she could do a little horse-trading. Gina missed out, all the same. Felicity and Justin had their famous row and all the house knew about the boy friend. Gina had wasted her bread."

" How do you know all this?" Mel demanded.

Aubrey grinned.

" I have my methods! A lot of funny things have been happening around here and I'm keeping my eyes open. Did you know that both Dominic and Justin went out in the early hours of the morning, a few days ago? I don't know why, yet, but I'm working on it."

A dreadful foreboding seized Mel.

" When, exactly?"

" A couple of days before Christmas. Night of the twenty-second. Morning of the twenty-third, to be exact. Mean anything to you?" he added, eagerly.

The night Melissa died. But that was out at sea. The unexplained journey could have nothing to do with that.

She shook her head.

" I don't think so. Were they together?"

" Nope. Dominic went first, Justin ten minutes later."

" How can you know that?"

" The watchman had to open the gates for the cars, didn't he?"

Outside in the hall, the telephone rang. Aubrey sprang up and ran out.

" I'll get it," Mel heard him call to the servant come in response to its summons. " Hey, Mel, it's for you."

Once again, she hastened to answer, this time hoping it might be Justin. And again, it was Mrs. Nelson. But this time, she was not angry or aggrieved. She was crying.

" They've found him out on the reef," she sobbed. " They say he has been dead for days. And me saying all those no-good things about him!"

" What? Peter?"

" Drownded! Oh, Lordie! I'll never forgive myself."

" It isn't your fault."

" I bin thinking things! And him lying dead all the time. I tole him that beat-up old Bermudan cutter weren't sea-worthy."

" Was that his boat?"

" Not his. He didn't have no boat. It belonged to some feller he knew. They haven't found him yet, or the wreck, but the fishes have got them for sure. The police say I got to identify Peter. Honey, I don't reckon I can face that alone. I ain't got no folks here. I know its asking a lot, but could you come over?"

" Of course, I will," Mel replied impulsively, thinking only of the woman's distress. " It will take me a little while. I'll set out right away."

" Peter ain't going to go away," Mrs. Nelson sobbed.

It was only after she had hung up that it occurred to Mel that there might not be a car for her to drive, since she usually used Dominic's and he would have taken that to go into Kingston for the funeral. She went to the garage and discovered that there were no less than three to choose from: Vera's oversized American limousine, the modest, ancient saloon which Gina owned, and Felicity's shiny sedan, returned from police laboratory examination. The keys hung on numbered hooks on a board. Mel did not really want to ride in any of these cars, but there was no other way of fulfilling her rash promise to Mrs. Nelson. With a sigh, she selected Felicity's car.

The whole trip took a lot longer than she anticipated, but she was glad she had gone. Mrs. Nelson was in a pitiful state, the ordeal at the mortuary was frightful, and she felt obliged to stay with the poor woman until some of the horror had worn off. She even welcomed the excuse for lingering: the body had suffered damage from fish and from the sea while it lay on the reef, and Mel had never seen anything so terrible in her life. She thought it would haunt her dreams for years to come. It was dark before she reached Eagles' Nest. She stumbled into the house, feeling exhausted and sick.

And there was Justin, his face thunderous, standing in the doorway of the lounge.

" Where have you been?"

" Port Antonio," she said wearily. " Mrs. Nelson rang me. Peter Power has been found drowned. She had to identify him, and she didn't want to go alone. I couldn't refuse her. Her husband is dead, and her children are in England. She hasn't anybody, and she wishes she were back in

162

Birmingham."

As she spoke, his face softened to a mixture of exasperation and tenderness.

"Oh, Mel! You didn't run away, then?"

"Run away?" she echoed, not understanding. Vaguely, she was aware of other people crowding behind him in the doorway. One of them pushed Justin aside. It was Superintendent Marshall.

"I've men combing the island for you," he said shortly. "Even watching the airports. I thought you had bolted."

He started to move towards her but Justin was there before him. He put his arm round her protectively.

"She looks all in, Superintendent. Can't this keep for a while?"

"No. Please stand aside, Mr. French. For your information, Miss Grainger, Dominic Dewar is under arrest and I want you to come with me. Now."

Justin was still holding her.

"May I come too?"

"You may follow us, if you wish," Marshall conceded, and led Mel out to a waiting police car.

She expected C.I.D. Headquarters, but instead they were driven to the mortuary, a grim building, heavy with the presence of death. Why she had been brought here was beyond imagining.

There was a body to be viewed. The attendant pulled back the covering sheet, and Mel looked at the dead face of her twin sister. She recoiled, and Justin grasped her shoulders in a firm hold, as she swayed.

"You recognise this woman?" Superintendent Marshall demanded.

She nodded.

" My sister," she whispered, and felt Justin's hands tighten momentarily.

" The likeness is unmistakable," Marshall went on, " even though this young woman has been dead for a few days. Her passport was on her and the photograph in that is quite remarkable. It could be you. Are you identical twins?"

" Yes."

" According to the passport, she is Melinda Grainger, a teacher, and she appears to have arrived in Jamaica on December eighteenth. Is that correct?"

" Not quite," said Justin, and his hands dropped from her shoulders. His voice was harsh. " I think you will find that it is the other way round. She is Melinda. It is Melissa who is dead."

" Is that so, Miss Grainger?"

" Yes. I'm Melinda." She turned to look imploringly at Justin, but his face was forbidding. " It was one of Dominic's experiments. To see if one twin could take the other's place without detection."

He turned away from her, and she thought the earth under her feet shook.

She was taken to the C.I.D. office for questioning.

" There is no point in continuing any further pretence," Superintendent Marshall told her sternly. " I have known for days that a young woman answering your description was seen in Port Antonio on the day that Felicity Dewar was murdered. The stumbling block has been your alibi, also the fact that I could find no rental company which had hired a car to her. Mr. Morley is here. Do you wish to talk to him before making any statement that may incriminate you?"

Mel shook her head.

"I'll tell you everything I know. I can't tell you where Melissa got that car. I don't know. You will find it at a garage somewhere near the Planters' Inn, which is some miles along the coast, west of Port Antonio. Melissa drove it there on the day of the murder. She was joining a friend for a cruise in his yacht. You should be able to find the wreckage of it somewhere near the spot where she was washed up. It's a beautiful thing called a Tradewind and the owner is a man named Jim Brown. I suppose he is drowned, too."

Marshall subjected her to a keen stare.

"Drowned?"

"Wasn't she?"

"No. She was strangled. She was found on the coast near the mouth of the Yallahs River, but she wasn't washed up. The body had not been in the water. Why did you assume she was drowned?"

"I shared her last moments. I knew she was at sea. I supposed it was a shipwreck."

"Telepathy between twins?"

"Yes."

"When?"

"Shortly after three in the morning on December twenty-third. It's not evidence in your sense, but you can take it from me, that is when it happened."

"You seem to be on my side, all of a sudden," Marshall commented thoughtfully.

"You can't do anything to Melissa now. She's dead. I don't believe she conspired with Dominic to kill his wife, but I accept that she—and I—may have been used, without our knowledge."

"Your loyalty does you credit, but it blinds you. There

165

is no question that your sister was inside the French beach house. Her fingerprints match the unidentified set we found there, and the key was in her pocket. So Miss Grainger, let us start at the beginning and go through this step by step.'

It was a long session, coming at the end of a tiring day. Mel felt herself beyond exhaustion. She lost track of time, even of people. At intervals, Tib Morley was there, and for long periods she was left alone, except for a watchful policewoman, in an interrogation room. Then, incredibly, Tib was there again, with his hand under her arm, leading her out into the warm night.

"They are letting me go?" she asked, in wonder.

"For the moment. Superintendent Marshall inclines to the view that you were an innocent tool. It doesn't mean that you won't be charged eventually."

"And Dominic?"

Tib shook his head.

"He's in trouble. You will be the star witness against him. You have put him right on the spot by giving Marshall the moment when Melissa died. Dominic was away from Eagles' Nest at the critical time."

"Aubrey said Justin followed him."

"Trust that boy to know! I wonder what else he has under his thatch? Dominic's story is that there was a phone call, around two that morning, from some man who said he had information about Felicity's murder, and wanted Dominic to meet him at Gunboat Beach on the Palisadoes. Only there was no one there, though he waited until four. Justin can confirm the phone call. He took it, and switched it through to Dominic at the guest cottage. But he can't alibi him. He heard Dominic leave, decided to go after him, but by the time he had flung on some clothes and fetched

166

his car, he was a good ten minutes behind him. He didn't catch him before he reached the main road, and then there was no means of telling which way Dominic had gone. But you see, Mel, the place where Melissa was killed is only about half an hour's drive from Eagles' Nest. So Dominic is right in the cart. I don't blame you for telling the police everything you know—it's your only way of saving yourself—but you can be too bloody co-operative!"

They reached the street, and at the curb was a familiar Mercedes, with Justin himself at the wheel.

"Get in," he said, curtly.

He drove home at a furious pace, in a silence which Mel found more daunting than any amount of recriminations. Once in the house, she thought to escape directly to her room, but he grasped her wrist and drew her into the big, deserted lounge.

"Why, Melinda?" he asked, still holding her. "I keep kicking myself for not guessing. I knew you were different. Melissa lived in my house for four months, and I didn't even like her much. Not until a few days ago, when suddenly I found myself attracted. Only it wasn't her, it was you. From what I have learnt of you since, you aren't the sort of person to act irresponsibly, much less to connive at a murder. You are warm and you care about people. So, *why* did you ever agree to this mad scheme?"

"You can't know how I'm regretting it. If I hadn't come here, Melissa would still be alive. And there is a good chance that Felicity and Gina, too, wouldn't be dead, either. How do you think I feel about that?"

"It's too late to be sorry," he shot back, harshly. "Melinda, there has to be truth between us. Why did you do it?"

167

" I was tired, and lonely, and I was afraid, too. What I told you about looking after my parents is true. Dad died in October. Melissa's letter came right after the funeral. We hadn't heard from her in years. She and Dad had a terrible row, and she walked out. It was over a boy friend. He worked in London, and she got a job there, too, and moved into his flat. My father couldn't accept the permissive society, nor could he believe that one of his daughters was living with a man. I tried to find Melissa when Mum died, but she was gone without trace."

" And that was what brought you here?"

" There was something else. When my mother died, I was engaged. His name was Scott and he was more or less the boy next door. He is an engineer, and he was offered a plum job in Africa. He wanted me to go with him, but I couldn't abandon Dad. He was in a shocking state. I needed a few months to get him settled, with somebody to look after him, or, at worst, in a home. Scott made an issue of it: either I went with him at once, or I didn't love him enough. He was right: I didn't!"

" So you broke it off and he went alone?"

" Oh, no. The next thing I knew, he had married my best friend and taken her to Africa. She jumped at the opportunity. They are home on leave, this Christmas. I didn't want to see them. Melissa offered me a chance to run away and I took it."

He let go her wrist, and pulled her into his arms.

" Are you still pining for Scott?"

" You know I'm not," she said, and put her face up for his kiss.

" There will be some cold supper on the dining-room table," Justin said, some time later. " I'm hungry. I thought

168

Superintendent Marshall was never going to be through with you."

"You were there all the time?"

"Every blessed moment. You don't think I could have come back home, while you were being held in that place? Come on. Let's see what George has put out for us."

"I couldn't eat!"

"Nonsense. You are a healthy young woman. You have had a terrible day, but it's over now. You are in the clear."

"How can I be?"

"Tib says you will make an excellent witness. Any jury would believe you."

"And Dominic?"

"There is not much we can do for him," Justin said soberly. "Tib will do his best, but I do not see how we can save him. Or if he is worth saving! We have to accept the fact that he hired Melissa and her boy friend to kill Felicity. Melissa has paid her debt. We don't know where Jim Brown is. He must have set Melissa ashore, phoned Dominic to tell him where to pick her up, and sailed away with a pocketful of dollars—if he's lucky!"

"Lucky?"

"I mean, if Dominic hasn't killed him too. Melinda, don't you realise what a narrow escape you have had? You were always the most potentially damaging witness against him. Thank God he has been stopped before he could attack you."

It was only when she was on the verge of sleep that a thought popped up through the barbiturate-induced haze: Why hadn't Dominic tried to kill her?

TWELVE

The question was still with her in the morning, but in the meantime, her subconscious mind had produced an answer: Dominic Dewar had made no attempt on her life because he had killed no one. Not Felicity, nor Melissa, nor Gina. It came to her that there was a good reason why she had been left alive while others had been struck down: she was meant to speak, and every time she opened her mouth, she made matters worse for Dominic.

So who was behind it all?

"Back to Square One, if you are right," said P.J. O'Donnell, into whose ear she poured her thoughts. He was the only person around the house to whom she could talk. Justin had gone into Kingston before she was up, Aubrey was having another session with the Narcotics Division and Mr. Wartburg had departed to take a plane back to New York, which left only Vera, and Mel had no desire to confide in her.

"I must be right," she insisted. "There is altogether too much evidence against Dominic. He has been set up. Framed. Take the weapon, for instance. Why use a harpoon from the beach house? Why bother to put it back afterwards? Pointers to Dominic, who else? And here's something else: the only thing that has stood between Dominic and instant arrest, from the moment of finding Felicity's body, has been

170

his alibi for the day of the murder. That would be valueless the moment the existence of my twin sister was revealed. Yet Melissa made no attempt to cover her tracks on the day of the murder. She called on Mrs. Nelson, and she went to the Planters' Inn. And when the body was found, in her pocket was my passport, and the key of the beach house. Dominic and Melissa couldn't have been that stupid!"

"Then what do you think happened?" P.J. inquired. "What about this Jim Brown?"

"He must have been the one to fire that spear at Felicity, but I don't believe that Melissa was there when he did it, or that Dominic hired Jim to do it. Melissa took her time that day. I doubt if she went anywhere near the beach house. The police found her fingerprints on one of the changing-room doors but they could have been there for weeks. And the key that was found on her was a plant, for sure. I'll bet she was wasn't on Jim's boat much before evening. Then they cruised round the coast and came ashore in the early hours of the morning, about thirty-six hours after Felicity died. Jim phoned Dominic, to get him away from the house, so that he would have no alibi, and then killed Melissa, making sure that she would be identified the moment she was found."

"It hangs together," P.J. agreed. "But if Dominic didn't hire Jim Brown, who did? The choice isn't very wide. Whoever it was must have known about you taking Melissa's place, and must have killed Gina, too, because she found out something and was putting the bite on them. Someone in this house, and the normal population is diminishing."

"It has to be Vera. She put on a good show of grief for her niece, but she was on the stage once, and there is only one person she really cares for, and that is Aubrey. Felicity

171

had uncovered a fearful scandal about him. He might be sent to prison for years. Vera would do anything to protect him. And she could have handed over the key of the beach house to Jim Brown. She won't say where she was on the morning of the murder."

"I was in a stinking muddy sugar-cane field, paying money to a stinking little blackmailer," said a voice from behind them.

Mel and P. J. looked round, startled. Sitting under a large umbrella at the side of the pool, they had not heard Vera approach across the grass.

"I seem to be the only person in the house who wasn't told that my son has confessed to the police that he smuggled drugs. I'm only his mother, of course," she said bitterly. "I'm going into town now, to lay information against that little runt who has been squeezing me. He's the one Aubrey handed the stuff over to, and I'm going to make sure he gets sent down with the rest of them. And as for you, Melissa —no, I'm wrong, it's Melinda, isn't it?—I'm sorry for you."

"Sorry for me? Why?"

"You are in love with Justin. I saw that days ago. He will marry you, if only to make sure that you never understand the truth."

"What truth?"

"That he had Felicity killed."

Mel jumped up.

"What?"

Vera put out a hand as if to hold her off.

"Listen to me! You are right, there is too much evidence against Dominic. But I didn't set him up, and that only leaves Justin. I don't want to believe it, because I loved his father, and I have always had respect for him. And there is

172

no way that we can prove it. He has been too clever for us. You and I are going to have to live with it. What are you going to do? Go home to England? Or marry a murderer?"

Mel felt her legs shaking under her. She reeled back into her chair.

"I won't believe it!" she exclaimed desperately. "Why on earth should Justin want to get rid of Felicity? He hardly knew her."

"Is that what he told you? Then let me put the record straight. When Justin was at Oxford, he was engaged to her. She broke it off, and he has never looked at a woman since. He was very upset when we heard about Dominic's marriage. I was staggered when he invited them to stay here. Now we know why, don't we? If you don't believe me, ask yourself if Dominic would play such a big trick as substituting you for Melissa without asking Justin's permission first. Whoever killed Felicity had to know about that so that Dominic could be set up as the fall guy. Justin is the only person Dominic would have told."

Vera turned on her heel and walked into the house. A few moments later, there was the sound of her car in the drive, and then silence.

P.J. let out a low whistle.

"How's that for a turn-up for the book? Are you really in love with him?"

Mel had her hands to her face. Tears ran down between her fingers. She nodded, unable to speak.

It fitted together like the pieces of a Chinese puzzle. No stranger had ever been able to tell her and Melissa apart, so why should Justin have that power? The answer was that he had not. He *knew*, and all the rest followed from it. She

173

could see it so clearly, and it seemed that the world had come to an end.

Clouds blotted out the sun, blowing up black from the sea. Within minutes, large drops of rain began to fall. P.J. pulled her to her feet and together they ran into the house, as the sudden tropical storm came thundering down.

In the hall, the telephone began to ring. The bell shrilled on and on, until Mel roused herself enough to answer it.

" I can't think where George is," she remarked, as she left the lounge.

" In town, I think," P.J. called out, behind her. " And the maids are upstairs."

Mel hesitated to pick up the handset, fearing that it might be Justin, and wondering how she could bear to hear his voice. Instead, a by-now-familiar Jamaican voice came through.

" Oh, Mrs. Nelson," she said, relieved. " How are you today?"

" I don't know whether I'm on my head or my heels, honey. That poor Peter didn't die natural. He was held under the water, and fought hard. Policeman says there's the murderer's skin under his fingernails, and they is going to find him."

Mel took a deep breath.

" Do they know who?"

" It must be that Jim Brown, the one whose boat he went out in."

" Did you say, *Jim Brown?*"

" That's right. Honey, I'll have to go. The police is here again. I'll call you later."

" Yes, do that," said Mel faintly.

She went back to the lounge. P.J. looked up expectantly.

174

" Anything interesting?"

" Oh, yes. That was Mrs. Nelson. She says Peter Power was murdered. And guess what? The police are looking for the friend who took him out in his boat. One Jim Brown."

" The same?"

" It must be. There wouldn't be two white men of that name in a place like Port Antonio. Funny, I thought Jim Brown's boat was a yacht called a Tradewind. Mrs. N. said it was an old Bermudan cutter. Superintendent Marshall is looking for the wrong boat, but I suppose the Port Antonio people will put him right."

" When do they think Peter was killed?"

" She didn't say. It would be difficult to establish, I should think, with him lying out on the reef for days. He went out with Jim the day before Felicity was killed. You know, P.J., I think we are all wrong about Peter. I don't think he was Felicity's boy friend at all. Dear God! it was Justin who told me that he was. And I accepted it because I saw a photograph of Felicity in Peter's room. But Gina had hired someone in Port Antonio to take shots of her. Heavens! I knew there was something odd about that robbery."

" What robbery? You've lost me."

" Peter's room was burgled, but I saw cameras in there, valuable things, and the thieves hadn't touched them. So what did they want?"

" The photographs of Felicity and the mysterious boy friend," P.J. said, promptly. " Mel, you do realise who it has to be, don't you?"

She nodded, speechless. Justin! The clandestine lover and the father of the unborn child.

The whole universe seemed to have collapsed about her head. Outside the storm raged, and lightning cracked the sky, but Mel did not hear it.

"That's why Felicity wanted to buy that yacht," she said, miserably, wishing her mind would not work so clearly. It presented a stream of damning facts like the frames of a ciné film seen one at a time. "It was a present for him."

Once more she was called to the telephone. This time it was Justin, and his voice seemed to come from a long distance, almost drowned out by the roaring in her ears. She was obliged to hand the phone to P.J. to complete the call.

"He's worried about you. He asked me if you were ill. I said you didn't like the storm. He says the road is flooded. We are cut off up here, until it goes down. Mel, what are you going to do about Justin?"

"I don't know. I just want to go away. Anywhere."

She was even thankful for the flooded road. At least, it would keep Justin away from here for some hours.

"Wishing you were back in Bradford?" P.J. inquired, sympathetically.

Mel nodded. Then it occurred to her that no one here knew she lived in Bradford. She had never mentioned the place to anyone. Not even to Justin.

"How did you know—?"

The ringing of the telephone interrupted her, and she ran into the hall to answer it, her head full of questions.

A tiny little voice told her to hold the line for a call from New York. Then someone else asked for Dominic, and she offered to take a message, reaching for the pad and pencil kept by the phone.

It was short and staggering. Her mind raced as the implications crowded in on her. Most of all, she felt a boundless relief: Justin was himself, not the vicious, scheming hypocrite of her imagination. More, he was the one living

176

soul who knew her from Melissa without being told. The one man in the world for her.

" What was that?" asked P.J.

She turned round slowly. He was standing in the doorway of Justin's study.

He had caught her unawares, before she had had time to digest the new information or to arrange her face into neutral lines.

" You know!" he said incredulously. " I thought you might, just now, but it didn't seem possible. How the divil did you do it?" He brought his hand up from his side, and her horrified eyes took in a wicked-looking pistol. " Justin's weapon. Ironical, isn't it? Kind of him to keep it in his desk where anyone who needs it can get at it! Into the lounge, Melinda. You and I have to talk."

Slowly, she obeyed the movement of the gun. It wasn't real, it couldn't be—but there was something dreadfully convincing about that pistol, and the eyes in the pointed leprechaun face did not waver. She wondered how she could ever have thought him droll.

" P.J.," she whispered. " Please!"

Her knees shook. She knew with a frightful certainty that he was going to kill her. It was all so unfair! A moment ago she had seen a bright future open up before her. Now this little jerk was going to blow it all to pieces.

" Sit down, Melinda. Over there, and put your hands in your lap. Now, me darlin', you talk and I'll listen. First, what put you onto me?"

" You shouldn't have known about Bradford. All they know here is that I come from England. Only Melissa could have told you."

" Is that *all*?" he demanded, stunned. " What was that

177

phone call, just now?"

Keep him talking, she thought. Keep him talking and perhaps help will come. Please come! Anyone! she prayed. Justin! But fear seemed to be blocking her mental processes. The only face which swam into her mind was that of Manley, of all people.

P.J. was waiting for an answer.

" A friend in New York. Dominic asked him to find out who owned Tradewind yachts on this side of the Atlantic," she said hastily. "We thought Jim had one. Melissa was always speaking of that type of yacht. She didn't sail herself, so she must have had it from her boy friend."

" So?"

" Felicity was interested in a Tradewind, too. She sent for the brochure. I should have known that she would not have got the idea from listening to Melissa's chatter about the yacht. They weren't on those sort of terms. So where did she hear of it? From her own boy friend. But it is too much of a coincidence. Two men both keen on a new English yacht. So it has to be one boy friend for the pair of them, seeing Felicity during the week and Melissa at the weekends. Jim Brown."

" What does that prove?"

" Dominic's friend says there is only one of those yachts sold to someone over here. A man by the name of David Astley, in Nelson's Harbour, Antigua. Your friend. I suppose that was what you crossed in?"

P.J. smiled ferociously.

" Me and my big mouth. Yes, I crewed for him in his new Tradewind. I never thought Melissa would take in that much about boats. She wasn't very bright, your sister. She never imagined that while I dated her at weekends, I spent

178

the rest of the time with Felicity."

"Who would? It was very clever of you," Mel said deliberately. She thought she saw through the open door a shadow in the hall. Keep him talking, she reminded herself. "How did you turn yourself into Jim Brown?"

"It was easy. I told David I was going to spend a few weeks on Barbados, and persuaded him to cover for me in case the family asked. I was supposed to be doing a bit of honest work for him! I flew in here, hired that old Bermudan cutter in Kingston, sailed round to the north coast, and set myself up in Ocho Rios, where I could merge with all the other craft. I was living on the boat, and no one was going to ask for my passport if I stayed in Jamaican waters."

She was sure there was someone out in the hall now. Above everything, she must keep P.J.'s attention on her.

"What gave you the idea in the first place?"

He smiled his old charming grin, except that now it was like the face of the crocodile.

"I felt I'd been cheated. Old man Farrell was going to leave my Ma and Uncle Stephen a good slice of bread, but he died too soon. My Ma wouldn't have handed any over to a layabout like me, but Uncle Stephen is on his last legs, so I shouldn't have had to wait long. I don't want to spend my life in a dusty old solicitors' office. I was wondering how I could help myself when Dominic's letter came. It seemed a strange coincidence that they were leaving for the Caribbean at just about the same time as myself."

"How did you meet Felicity? and Melissa?"

"The good luck was on my side. I fell in with Peter Power—by the way, no cousin of mine. I invented that for a little diversion—and he led me to Melissa. She was just what I wanted. Getting to Felicity was easy after that. Then Melissa told me you were coming, and I saw it all open up in front of me."

"How did you do it?"

"Easy as kiss your hand! I arranged to meet Felicity at the beach house on the day you and Dominic would be at the conference. It amused me to let the pair of you have an alibi. It would make it so much more effective when Melissa's body was found to blow it all sky high. I had borrowed an old banger from a chap at a garage near the Planters' Inn for Melissa to drive over. I wanted her journey to be traceable, when the time came, and I asked her to drop in on Mrs. Nelson with a message for Peter. Not that he could have received it, poor fellow. He was out on the reef, where I had left him the day before. It was a pity about Peter."

"You killed him because of the photographs?"

"I had to. He was the only one who could connect me with Felicity. I broke into his place and got the negatives and all the prints—or so I thought, until that interfering little bitch Gina recognised me. She had already had a set from Peter. So she had to go, too."

Mel shivered. He was a monster. She prayed that whoever was out in the hall would come in, preferably with a small army behind him.

"Tell me about Felicity."

"I'd told her we would go scuba diving, if she could borrow some equipment. So there she was, waiting at the landing stage outside the beach house, with a couple of guns and harpoons. We sailed round to the creek for a bathe, first. I never even set foot there, in case I left a print. I stood in the cutter's dinghy and shot her. Then I sailed back to the beach house, replaced the equipment, and on to the Planters' Inn to pick up Melissa.''

"Why did you have to kill her, too?"

P.J.'s eyebrows rose.

"I should have thought that didn't need explaining to a bright girl like you. I needed her dead to bust Dominic's alibi. I picked my spot on the south coast, far enough from Kingston to be remote, near enough to Eagles' Nest for Dominic to have done the job.''

"And you made that phone call?''

"I did. And very neatly it worked, too.''

"But why involve Dominic? He had never done anything to you.''

"I needed a fall guy," P.J. said casually. "As a sort of insurance policy. So that the police would be happy. They don't like unsolved murders. They have him for Gina's murder, too. I borrowed a pair of his slacks and a shirt. There's a nice smear of blood on each.''

Suddenly, he strode across to her, grabbing her wrist and forcing her out of her chair.

"Walk in front of me now, like a good girl," he said, twisting her arm behind her so that she had no choice, and cried out in pain. "Over to the door. I think we have company.''

Mel's heart sank. Under his direction, she stumbled across the room.

"Come in, whoever you are," said P.J. "Slowly. Or the girl dies now.''

There was a moment's pause, then Norman Manley Robertson walked in. Mel stared at him, her mind blank with shock. Only minutes ago his face had flashed across her mind and now he was here.

181

"And who is this?" P.J. demanded.

"He's George's son," Mel told him.

"Lucky for me I caught sight of him in that mirror over there. No doubt he was hoping to surprise me. All right, over there on that settee, both of you."

Hope ebbed. Manley was alone, and they were both unarmed. And P.J. was going to kill the pair of them.

"Bad luck for you, my friend, to come into the house just at that moment. You will have to go the same as Melinda. Another tragedy in the garden, as soon as that infernal rain stops."

"Manley, why did you come?" she murmured.

He was sitting bolt upright, staring at P.J.

"May I take off my glasses?"

Melinda jumped. It was such an odd request, at once irrelevant and out of character. Those dark glasses seemed to grow on Manley's face.

"Be my guest," said P.J. "But do it slowly. And don't try any tricks. I'm handy with pea-shooters."

Manley took off the sunglasses.

"I came because you called me," he said to Mel, and turned to look at her. She saw what the glasses had hidden : he had the same strange eye as his father. The product of Castro's Cuba was a Four-Eyed One.

P.J. laughed softly.

"She didn't call! Come on, admit you were snooping!"

But she had called. She had sent out the sort of mental message which in the past would have told Melissa that she was needed. She had hoped to reach Justin. Instead, Manley had picked up the wave.

"You can't get away with killing us, too," Mel said firmly.

182

P.J. laughed once more.

"Oh, but I shall! Vera will testify that you were overcome by the thought that Justin might be a murderer, and I shall give a heart-rending account of how I saw our black friend try to stop you shooting yourself, but failed, of course, and got shot himself for his pains. There is nothing to connect me with Jim Brown, Felicity's murderer—not even the cutter. That's scuttled in deep water off Port Royal, one amongst hundreds of wrecks—and for the tragedies in this house P.J. O'Donnell is no more than a casual bystander."

"I don't know how you had the nerve to come here!" Mel gasped. "I would never have made the connection otherwise."

"And you are the only one that will. Bad luck on you! It wasn't my original intention to return to Jamaica," P.J. admitted, with a smile. He was enjoying himself hugely. "But when my Ma's cable arrived, I couldn't resist the temptation. It was a challenge I couldn't ignore. And she sent me the fare, too. What's the matter with him?"

Manley had begun to sway slowly backwards and forwards. From his lips issued a low crooning note.

"How should I know? You intend to kill us both. Perhaps he is making his peace with his gods. Does it bother you?"

P.J. shook his head.

"Nothing bothers me, me darlin'. Everything is just as I want it."

There was no way of shaking his confidence. Mel listened to the rain still beating down outside, and tried to will it to go on for ever, even though she knew it must add to the floods on the road which would prevent Justin from coming home. She began to appreciate the true meaning of the phrase 'While there's life, there's hope". She would go on hoping until the moment that he pulled the trigger.

P.J. did not seem to want to talk any more, his ready tongue still for once. Apart from the rain, the only sound was Manley's crooning. Gradually, it seemed to fill the room . . .

Then, incredibly, P.J.'s grip on the pistol slackened, momentarily. He tightened it, but in another few minutes, his hand dropped again. The gun slipped from his fingers and skidded across the floor. P.J. stood watching it, unmoving.

Manley rose to his feet in one swift, smooth movement. In two strides he had reached P.J. who looked up at him, like one in a dream.

" Get the gun, Miss Grainger," Manley said quietly, and Mel dived for it.

" What has happened to him?" She whispered.

" He will come round very soon. I have turned his eye. In your terminology, it is a form of hypnosis."

" You are a Myalman."

" I was trained to it as a child," he acknowledged. " My forebears were priests in Ashanti from the time that the nation began." Hurriedly, as if regretting the admission, he replaced his dark glasses. " I have rejected all that, Miss Grainger."

" Oh, no, you haven't. You've saved both our lives. How can you say you have rejected it?"

" I would rather have had an automatic rifle! However, I was unarmed, so I had to use what weapons I had to hand. I must ask you not to spread the story all over Kingston. My reputation would be ruined."

" Don't you believe it! You would be made for life. You said, you heard me call you. I was trying to send a message to Justin. How did you pick it up?"

" I, too, am telepathic. Like you with your sister. The elders call it ' talking to the spirits '. If it works properly, help should be here soon. I sent a message to my father the same way."

The rain had stopped, but there was a new sound outside the house. Man-made sound. Mel ran to the window. Two helicopters were setting down in front of the house. Justin jumped out of the first and ran towards the front door, with George at his heels. Superintendent Marshall climbed out of the other.

The room filled with men, but Mel was hardly aware of them. Justin's arms were round her, holding her as if he would never let her go.

" Melinda, my darling, I thought we might be too late. I knew there was something wrong when I spoke to you on the phone. I was scaring up a chopper to bring me up here when George burst in, saying the spirits had told him you were in danger."

She clung to him.

" I was so afraid it was you," she sobbed into his shoulder. " Vera said Felicity had jilted you and you had never got over it."

" Vera is an ass. I was the one who broke it off. She was the girl I told you about. She was in the process of getting rid of her first husband then. I didn't even know she was married until that Wartburg arrived in London to tie up the legal ends of her divorce. He took it very badly that I wouldn't give up either the family business or my religion to please his best friend's little girl, but what he really

185

couldn't forgive was that I wasn't a poor struggling student thankful to marry an heiress. I was well out of that lot and I knew it, but I will admit that it made me wary of women."

The room was clearing now. P.J. had been taken away, and Superintendent Marshall had finished talking to Manley. He cleared his throat impatiently.

" Miss Grainger!"

Justin relaxed his hold on her.

" I'm told that O'Donnell made a complete confession to you?"

" If you can call it that. It was more in the nature of a gloat."

They went into Justin's study for her to make a statement while it was all fresh in her mind.

" Will that stand up in court?" she asked when it was finished.

" There will be plenty of other evidence to back it up," Marshall assured her. " He could fool his friends on Antigua that he was going only to Barbados, but that is where you change planes to fly on to Jamaica. It's usually an overnight stop, so he could even make fancy arrangements with one of the hotels to take messages. No doubt he did. We shall be able to track him there, and through his onward flights. He would have to use his own passport. And we can find that Bermudan cutter he hired. The man who owns it will be able to make an identification of him as ' Jim Brown '. Don't worry, Miss Grainger, you won't be making a fool of yourself when you stand up in court. There is a lot of work to be done, and I doubt if we shall be ready to take this case to trial for at least a couple of months. You understand you will have to return to Jamaica for it?"

" She'll be here," said Justin. " I will be taking her to
186

England to clear up her affairs and do whatever is necessary to resign her teaching position. Then she will be coming back here to live."

Superintendent Marshall permitted himself an unofficial comment.

" I thought she might," he said.

WOLVERHAMPTON
PUBLIC LIBRARIES